The Taste of Smoke

Poetry by Stacy Tuthill

PENNYROYAL (SCOP Publications) 1991
with teachers' guide.

NECESSARY MADNESS (University of Alaska, Fairbanks) 1992.

The Taste of Smoke

Stories about Africa

Stacy Johnson Tuthill

I want to thank the Maryland State Arts Council for a Works-in-Progress grant in 1987-88 which made the completion of this manuscript possible. I also want to thank Joyce Renwick, Carol Hoover, and Jean Johnson for editorial advice and encouragement which made it possible for me to share these stories with a larger audience.

The following stories in THE TASTE OF SMOKE previously appeared in the following publications: "Battle of the Bees" in *A Loving Voice: A Caregiver's Book of Read-Aloud Stories for the Elderly*, edited by Carolyn Banks & Janis Rizzo, The Charles Press, Philadelphia, 1991; "Celebration," in *Lite Magazine*, as a winner in Lite Magazine's stort story contest, Annapolis, Maryland, Summer 1990, Vol 1, No.3; "A Test of Power," in *Pig Iron: Third World* (International edition), No.15, 1988. "The Proposal" was a Pen Syndicated Fiction winner, 1986, resulting in publication in *The Village Advocate*, Chapel Hill, NC, Nov. 2, 1986. "The Proposal" was first published in *New Writing from Zambia*, Spring 1974.

All photography, including the mask on the cover, is by the author.
The book was typeset and designed by Barbara Shaw.

ISBN 0-9637290-1-2
Library of Congress Catalog Catalog Card No. 94-72440

First Edition
Printed in the United States of America

EAST COAST BOOKS
P.O. Box 15132
Chevy Chase, Maryland 20825

Contents

*This book is dedicated to Dean,
Tom, Laura, Teresa and David*

Preface

My first African experience began in the summer of 1964 when my husband, Dr. Dean F. Tuthill, professor at the University of Maryland, made an intensive research study of shifting agriculture in the Eastern Province of Zambia, then Northern Rhodesia. The country was seething with excitement at the time. Zambia was preparing for independence in October of 1964, and government power was being transferred to Kenneth Kaunda with no bloodshed and a minimum of conflict. We returned eight years later for a year when Dean was awarded a Fulbright Scholarship to work at the African Studies Institute. We lived in an old British colonial house, the setting for "Battle of the Bees." Over the years my husband made a number of short consulting trips alone but worked on a project sponsored by the Agency for International Development (A.I.D.) in Sierra Leone in the early 1980's where I joined him during the summer months. In 1987-88, we lived in Kenya where he taught at Egerton University. I had received a Works-in-Progress grant from the Maryland State Arts Council, and it was during that time I wrote the draft for most of the stories in ***The Taste of Smoke***.

We lived among the Chewa people in the Eastern Province of Zambia during our first trip in 1964 who practiced shifting agriculture, one of the oldest forms of cultivation and found only in remote areas. Sometimes called "slash and burn," shifting agriculture involves burning and clearing a small area of land, cultivating it until its fertility is exhausted, and then leaving the soil to regenerate naturally while farmers move to a new area. The village was in the back-country about twenty miles from Fort Jameson, now Chipata, and could be reached only by a path in a sturdy Land Rover. We had no idea what we might find as no major anthropological studies were published until the following year when M.G. Marwick published ***Sorcery in Its Social Setting***, 1965, with the University of Manchester, England. While there, we lived in villages, in tents, or unfinished huts. By living with the people, we were exposed to nuances of behavior, attitudes, customs, and traditions which, usually, only anthropologists have opportunities to experience.

Every household was studied with regard to agricultural crops and practices, family structures, relationships, customs, and attitudes, especially with regard to the division of labor. We soon found it beneficial for me to interview women as they would confide (through an interpreter) personal feelings and situations they would not share with men. The information obtained in this way was helpful as one purpose of the research was to determine social constraints to new and better ways of farming. I soon found resentment among women concerning the uneven work load imposed upon them—child bearing, food preparation, planting, hoeing, harvesting, and earning cash through the brewing of maize beer. It was considered a husband's job to prepare the land for cultivation, participate in some farming activities, and earn extra cash by seeking employment in towns or game parks.

The social structure was matrilineal, but this meant only that heredity was traced through the mother. Men were dominant in all decision-making, and women were expected to be obedient. Even though polygamy had been practiced as long an anyone could remember, women expressed bitterness about sharing husbands with other wives.

The characteristic I found most amazing was the lack of conflict or aggressive behavior, even among children. After reading Marwick's book, I learned "good" behavior was based on fear of sorcery. Ill feeling on the part of anyone in the village might cause "bewitching," manifested in the form of sickness or death. Any insult or carelessness with regard to a deceased relative might cause the same results. Villagers performed rituals to ward off evil and avoided persons or situations which might bring harm to them or their families. This aspect of their culture is suggested in some of the stories.

Within the huge continent of Africa, customs and living patterns vary greatly among countries and among tribes within the same country. Some of the customs and attitudes presented in these stories are general throughout Africa while others are specific to a small area. Other expatriates in Africa may find their experiences distinctly different from those revealed here depending upon whether they lived in the city, the village, or in the northern, southern, central, or western parts of the continent. Therefore, generalizations about Africa and Africans can be misleading; I can only write about my experiences and how I was affected by them.

Although customs vary, westerners who work or visit in Africa find the cultures fascinating and often develop strong attachments to the people; but adjustments can be difficult. The western work ethic and preoccupation with time are incompatible with most African cultures. Some of the stories in ***The Taste of Smoke*** shed light on these differences. The stories about Africans in this book are based on observations and authentic information. While some stories about Americans inside Africa are fictional, others are based on actual episodes developed as fiction with fictional characters.

Stacy Tuthill

Culture Shock

"Are you awake?" Donna whispered to Richard in the dark.

"Yes"

"Do you hear something?"

"Be quiet. Listen," he said. Donna knew from his strained whisper he was afraid.

She had awakened to the sound of a child crying. Then the clamor began with a long, low moan, almost inaudible at first, increasing in volume until it reached a peak of emotional intensity and relapsed into a rhythmic chant. Other voices joined the chorus, first low and soft, then loud, pulsating, and almost dying out before rising to another peak. The effect was unearthly. In her mind Donna saw visions of shadowy medicine men, rattling gourds, drums, psychic possession, and death. She shivered and breathed in short gasps while ominous sounds droned on through the night.

Richard had received a grant to make a study of primitive slash-and-burn agriculture in a remote village in the Eastern Province of Zambia. They had searched libraries for information on the Chewa tribe and found only one short article explaining how neighboring Ngoni were patrilineal and aggressive while the Chewa were matrilineal and peaceful. Before the British stopped tribal wars and raids, it said, the Chewa men stood in fields and wept while Ngoni warriors carried off their wives.

"Sounds safe enough," Richard had said. "Maybe they'll be hospitable."

They left Chipata one afternoon in early June, jolting along the graded clay roads the dry season had shriveled and ridged into a giant washboard. Their old Land Rover was packed with a tent, army cots, boxes of canned food, tins of crackers, and enough bananas and papaya to last a week. They took with them an Nyanja interpreter, Mbewe, and another passenger, Victoria, an attractive blonde Peace Corps worker just out of college who would teach for two years in the local school serving four villages. She had volunteered to ride in back among luggage, equipment, and cardboard boxes.

"I might as well get used to roughing it right now," Victoria said, bouncing over the tailgate of the Rover and settling herself among luggage and tent stakes.

Victoria was excited about her assignment and kept a stream of chatter going as they bumped along. She watched for birds, trying to identify them from a bird book she carried in her lap. When they passed a large baobab tree, its trunk smooth and grey as concrete, she squealed, delighted.

"You know what I read about the baobab tree?" she asked.

"What?" Donna said, knowing she was asking a rhetorical question and wanted to tell them something.

"I read that Africans say when God made the baobab, he got all mixed up and put the roots on top and that it has no rings so nobody can tell how old it is. They say that jillions of little birds and animals make their home in that big tree and that during the dry season elephants squeeze the pulp of the tree to get water. Isn't that something?"

Richard drove faster. It was getting late, and night falls suddenly near the equator. Donna looked back at Victoria whose breasts flopped with each vibration of the vehicle; she held on to them with both hands, a look of pain distorting her face. She was embarrassed when Donna looked back and saw what she was doing.

"If anything is loose," Donna said, "you'd better hang onto it."

They both laughed.

"I didn't know sitting in back would be this bad," Victoria said, shaking her head.

"Want to change places?" Donna asked.

"These roads are like a washboard," Victoria said. "You couldn't take this."

"Think I'm too old?"

"Of course not."

By late afternoon, they jolted up the path and rolled into the village which would be their home for the summer. The headman received them with polite caution. The headman's two wives, a delegation of curious onlookers, and a group of ragged children stared as if they might have come from another planet. While the headman told Richard where to set up the tent and supervised how it was done, his wives escorted Victoria to a tiny hut built especially for her. Men had made the frame of bamboo and women had smeared the sides with tan clay. Someone had drawn abstract designs in dark brown and ocher clay beside the grass door to welcome the new teacher.

Donna saw a woman building a fire among three smooth stones and scouted around the edge of the village to find stones and enough wood for her own cooking fire. She warmed a large can of stew for the evening meal and invited Victoria to join them.

"You sure are a gourmet cook," Victoria quipped. "I was awfully hungry."

"My mother always said the way to be a good cook was to let everybody get hungry," Donna said.

As they washed dishes on the tailgate of the Land Rover, a messenger walked up with a live chicken.

"This is a welcome gift from the headman," he said through Mbewe, the interpreter. It was a scrawny hen they had seen scratching and pecking in the village yard when they arrived.

Mbewe thanked the messenger and accepted the chicken for them.

"What will you do with it?" Victoria asked, her head tilted, looking at the thin, starved body.

"If we keep it alive during the night, we might attract leopards and hyenas to our tent," Richard mused.

"If we kill it now, we might offend the headman," Donna said. "What do you think we should do with it, Mbewe?"

The interpreter shook his head refusing to give advice. Finally, Richard wrung its neck and watched it flop about in death throes while hungry children looked on. Then Donna boiled water to scald the chicken. She and Victoria picked the feathers and stored the plucked chicken in a plastic container.

At sunset, a cold wind blew from the south, the result of a snow storm in South Africa. Mbewe announced he would ride his bicycle to his home village to get blankets, as they had brought sleeping bags only for themselves and the villagers had nothing to give him. He had barely disappeared down the path when Richard and Donna realized how vulnerable they were without a voice. After discussing in whispers what might happen in a crisis, they put out their cooking fire and climbed into sleeping bags for the night.

When the drumming began, Donna fumbled in the dark for the flashlight and looked at the square face of her watch. It was ten o'clock. Unzipping her sleeping bag, she crept to the flap of the tent and peered into darkness. The night was black. No moon, no stars, no wood fires were burning.

"What do you see?" Richard asked. His voice was hoarse.

"Nothing."

"Then come back to bed."

For a moment, the chanting maintained a moderate level. Stamping, drumming, and banging accompanied the monotonous chanting and clapping. Hands and sticks drummed rhythmically on metal pots, pans and hollow wood. The rattle of gourds and bamboo squares filled with maize kernels grated on night air. Warbling tones of ululating pierced their ears, menacing, threatening, in an atmosphere of ancient magic.

"Do you suppose we shouldn't have killed the chicken?" Donna whispered.

Richard paused, sounding uncertain. "I don't know," he said. "I wouldn't think so."

"Maybe they're angry about something we did," Donna said. "Or didn't do."

"Maybe"

"I think I remember reading somewhere that Africans don't expect us to know their customs."

"This might have nothing to do with us," Richard said.

"Do you have the Land Rover packed and ready to go?" Donna whispered.

"Yes," he whispered back. "I've locked our food and most of our equipment in the Land Rover to make more room in the tent, but maybe we should get dressed."

They dressed, making as little noise as possible.

"What about Victoria?" Donna asked. "If we have to go, we can't leave her here.

Richard didn't answer.

"I'll take the flashlight and get her," Donna said. "I think I can find my way. It's not far.

Richard reached for her in the dark and took the flashlight out of her hand. "Don't be silly," he said. "I'll go."

"No," Donna insisted. "We'll need you to drive the Land Rover. Neither of us could drive that stick shift on the left side of the road. Just be ready if anything happens."

Donna found her way in the dark without having to turn on the light. She stood by Victoria's door, calling her name softly.

"Come in." Victoria's voice came in a hoarse whisper. She was wide awake.

Donna turned on the flashlight when she went inside. "I thought you might be afraid," she said.

"I am." Victoria's teeth chattered with cold and fear.

"Come to our tent and stay with us until this is over. We might have to leave suddenly, and we wouldn't go without you."

"Thanks for coming," Victoria said, "but I'll stay here. This is the house they gave me."

"Don't be foolish," Donna said, annoyed. "We don't know how serious this might be."

"Thanks anyway," Victoria said. "I'm staying. I came here to teach."

Donna returned to the tent and sat cross-legged at the flap, waiting, thinking how obstinate young people can be. Her eyes couldn't discriminate between shadows and almost imperceptible impressions of light. She thought she saw someone standing watch about ten yards away. Her heart pounded, her toes grew numb in her heavy socks and her fingers ached from cold. She lost all sense of time. She felt helpless and trapped.

She startled at the sound of Richard turning over; nerve endings tingled all over her body.

Richard got out of bed and sat beside her at the flap of the tent.

"Get back in bed and keep warm," he said, his voice gentle with concern. "There's no need to make yourself sick."

"I can't sleep," she said.

"It doesn't matter. You can rest; you may need your strength tomorrow."

"Someone is watching us," she said.

"Are you sure?"

"No."

"Come on back to bed," he said, tugging at her arm.

She strained her eyes to see outlines of the person standing watch. She cupped her hand beaming the flashlight on her watch again. It was one-thirty. Her head ached from the pounding rhythm, screaming, ululating, and the strange vocal noises exaggerated by thin night air.

Richard went back to his sleeping bag. His concern touched her, but his forced complacency stirred her anger.

She heard footsteps padding across the village yard and men's voices low and drowsy. Tones of questioning and of explanations floated with the disembodied voices toward the chanting. She recognized the headman's voice.

"Something important is happening," Donna whispered. "They woke the headman. Do you think there's going to be trouble?"

"I don't know," Richard said, "but don't make any noise."

She wondered: Did we violate some sacred taboo when we killed the chicken by twisting off its head? Are we unwelcome in the village? Will people question us? Torture us? She recalled stories of missionaries who had been slaughtered as they slept in their beds. She refused to sleep; she'd always been a fighter and wouldn't take death lying down. The horrible pounding and chanting droned on through the night. Her sinuses began to drain. She wiped her nose on her sleeve and made small sniffing sounds. She knew Richard thought she was crying.

Donna's eyes drooped with the hypnotic throbbing of drums, but she wouldn't leave the flap of the tent. Her headache grew worse, her body shook with anxiety and the effects of cold. At four o'clock, the chanting trailed off into silence followed by the rustling of corn husks. Richard broke his silence by turning over in bed again; she knew he hadn't slept.

Just before dawn she saw people silhouetted against the horizon in the white light before morning. They were walking single-file with baskets on their heads. Women were leaving the village, but what about the men? Did that mean they might be attacked?

Morning dawned crisp and clear. The sun rose radiant above tangled trees and sifted through edges of thatched roofs suspended in halos against a clear sky. Slanting light glistened on a patch of bamboo turned pale gold by the dry season. A bantam rooster crowed once. Donna found it hard to believe anything terrible could happen on such a beautiful day. Then she saw the figure her fear had identified as a guard; it was nothing more than a pole with a basket of chives on top to keep safe from pecking chickens.

The village looked deserted except for a few children and the headman's elderly mother, until the headman came out of the bush carrying a spear. She and Richard rolled up their sleeping bags, tying them tight to keep out insects, and sat on the sides of the cots.

Victoria stuck her head in the flap of the tent.

"Come on in and join the party," Donna said, a touch of sarcasm in her voice.

"That was some party they had last night." Victoria giggled.

"I hope the interpreter comes soon," Richard said.

Donna and Victoria sat at the flap of the tent and watched Mbewe coming up the path on his bicycle. They went out to meet him. He arrived smiling, but when he saw them, his smile faded. Donna still looked blue from cold. Richard and Victoria were pale, wore dark circles under their eyes, and the weary expressions of people who hadn't slept.

"We heard a child crying last night," Donna said, not wanting to tell everything at once. "Please find out what's wrong."

Mbewe looked puzzled.

"If a child is sick," Richard said, "we'll take it to the clinic."

Without a word, Mbewe went to the headman's mother's hut and spoke in low tones. Although she was as elderly woman and crippled with arthritis, there was no mistaking the scolding he gave her.

When Mbewe returned, they waited for an explanation, but none came.

"Was the child sick?" Donna asked.

"No, the child was not sick, only crying.

"Are people angry with us for something we've done?"

"No, people are not angry."

"What's wrong, then?"

"A woman was sick, but she is no longer suffering."

"Who was sick?"

"Avalisa."

"Can we take her to the clinic?"

"She does not want to go."

"What's wrong with her?"

"Somebody bewitched her," he said, turning his head away. Donna looked at Victoria whose eyes were wide with curiosity.

"Who bewitched her?" Donna knew her question wasn't welcome, but she was determined to get to the bottom of the mystery.

"Nobody knows who bewitched her, but her husband ran away. He is afraid of her. She has no help with her children and grandchildren."

"How do people know she's bewitched?"

"She is seized by evil spirits and falls to the ground. Last night people in the village made noise to cast out devils."

Donna gazed into ashes from last night's cooking fire and murmured, "Be careful when casting out your devils that you don't cast out the best thing that's in you."

"What did you say?" Victoria asked with a puzzled frown.

"Nothing." Donna said. "It's something I read from Nietzsche, I think. But it wouldn't apply here. Everything is different. We have so much to learn."

Donna saw fear in Mbewe's eyes and knew he had told more than he wanted to tell. Still, that didn't explain the empty village.

"Where are all the people? she asked, spreading her arms in a sweeping motion toward the huts.

"The men have gone hunting for cane rats," he said.

"And the women?"

"They have gone to the grinding mill."

"But I saw them leave before daylight."

"Yes," he said. "The grinding mill is far."

"How far?"

"Many kilometers. They will walk until the sun is at the top of the sky. A man will grind their maize, and they will walk home. It may be dark before they get back to the village."

Donna looked at Richard but couldn't read his face. She went to the plastic canister and looked at the chicken. It was even more scrawny with the feathers removed, mostly bones with a little meat. She didn't think it would be good to eat but might make a palatable soup.

"Why don't we take the Land Rover to the grinding mill and give the women a ride home?" Victoria asked.

"I was thinking about that," Richard said, "but the two of you stay here. We'll need the room."

"While you're gone, Victoria and I will make chicken soup," Donna said.

After they left, Donna put the chicken on to boil while Victoria chopped onions and opened cans of vegetables. Then, Victoria fell asleep on Donna's cot, exhausted from tensions of the night.

Richard and Mbewe returned in early afternoon with baskets of maize tied precariously on top of the Land Rover packed with tired but smiling women.

"Mbewe," Donna called. "Will you help me deliver chicken soup to the headman and to each of the women who walked so far with little sleep,"

"Oh, no, Madam," Mbewe said. "The chicken was a gift to you. You must not return a gift."

"But I would like to share it," Donna said.

Mbewe looked uncomfortable. "If you send the headman food made from the chicken, he will be obliged to send you another gift."

"Why?"

"That is our custom. You never return a gift."

Donna opened her mouth to protest.

"He might have nothing more to give you," Mbewe said, "and he would feel shame."

"Let's save the soup to feed the children tomorrow while everybody is at work," Victoria suggested.

"Good idea," Donna said. "The nights are cold and the soup won't spoil."

That night the village was quiet. Everyone seemed to sleep soundly except Donna and Richard; they lay awake whispering to each other in almost total darkness. Donna was overwhelmed by a lingering unreality. She felt herself bewitched by last night's terror, the rhythm of drums, the chanting, ululating, and weird cries. Who would have thought a year ago that she would be lying in a tent in the middle of Africa frightened out of her wits? She felt her neck and chest itching like she might break out with a rash.

"I'm glad Mbewe is of the same tribe," Donna said. "He will have to be our voice, guide, and adviser when the next crisis arises."

"That's the problem," Richard said. "I don't like being dependent. I'm going to learn Nyanga in a hurry."

"And I'm going to miss Victoria when we go home." Donna yawned. "Her bravery and good humor put me to shame. She's quite a girl. She'll be a good teacher."

"Yeah," Richard said. "Quite a girl," but he was thinking of his work in the village and wondering how long it would take him to learn to deal with the customs and a culture so different from his own.

A Test of Power

Joseph Zulu returned to Kadende village in Eastern Zambia to live with his Uncle Alick following his graduation from the mission primary school. His teachers had estimated his age at seventeen; he was born the year the man-eating lion ravaged his village. His fine school record and pleasant disposition helped him get part-time work at the local game park. Although the priest at the school had offered him a scholarship for secondary school, he wanted to return to Kadende to marry Neliya as soon as he had saved enough money to pay for his bride.

Meanwhile, he slept in a hut in the center of the village with boys who had gone through puberty rites. He shared his quarters with two other boys and his friend and age-mate, Kakalulu, who also worked at the game park. At night he lay awake thinking of Neliya, the prettiest girl in the village. Her large dark eyes, faintly slanted above high cheek bones, were set in a perfectly oval face. Her breasts were just beginning to form, and she would soon be ready for marriage. She was the headman's grand-daughter through the womb of his first wife, Mwanda, and although it was too early to ask his family to make arrangements, he always knew Neliya would be his first and proper wife. His love for Neliya was so private, he didn't confide in anyone, not even Kakalulu. He hadn't counted on interference from a stranger like Sobo Mwale.

Sobo walked into Kadende one day wearing city clothes and a smug expression, claiming to be a distant cousin of the headman's matrilineal clan. Alick couldn't recall the kinship, but, as headman, he was afraid to risk angering the spirits of his matrilineal kin by insulting Sobo or refusing hospitality. He had no choice but to invite him to sleep in his kitchen hut.

When Sobo was asked about his home village, he folded his arms across his chest, smiled, and gave evasive answers interpreted as subtle threats to deprive the village of his presence if people didn't treat him well. After a week, Mwanda, Alick's first wife, responsible for serving meals to guests, complained about the extra work involved in preparing large amounts of nsima to satisfy Sobo's enormous appetite.

"I'm old and sick," she said to Alick, "and the man eats like a hippopotamus. Other wives must take their turn with this work." But Alick pretended not to hear.

By the end of the first month, village men came to Alick in a group to complain about Sobo's behavior.

"He struts about the village giving bad advice," said Maliseni who lived in the hut beside Alick. "This man isn't one of us."

Leaning on his cane, Dambuzo added, "He rests in my hammock while I work in the field with my wives. Do you think this is fair?"

Cipanda, Alick's youngest brother complained, "When he first came to the village, he borrowed money from me. He's not an honest man."

Kabamba explained that he had been asked to speak for all the men about Sobo's attempts to seduce their wives, adding that if Sobo didn't leave the village he would cause trouble.

He waited for an answer. Getting no response from Alick, he added, "Sobo boasts about important relatives in the government service in Lusaka. Why don't you ask him to go there to live?"

Alick, like his first wife Mwanda, was getting old, and he was tired of settling disputes in the village. Finding himself caught in a delicate situation, he listened, shifted his weight from one foot to the other, and promised to make a decision soon. Only Joseph knew, or thought he knew, why Sobo extended his visit. Sitting with men in front of Alick's house in late afternoon, while they drank beer and talked about village affairs, he watched Sobo's eyes, bright with lust, follow Neliya as she knelt to serve nsima or ran errands for her grandmother. Joseph grew restless with anger. He was even more angry when he saw that Neliya seemed to enjoy Sobo's attention. She exaggerated the swing of her hips when she went to the well for water. She carried heavy loads on her head to show her great strength, and she turned downcast eyes in Sobo's direction when she thought nobody was looking. This was the kind of attention Neliya had given him before Sobo came to the village.

Joseph didn't know how to deal with the terrible feelings stirring inside. Both his grandfather and the missionaries had taught him that killing a man was bad, but he knew in his heart he wanted to rid the village of Sobo even if he had to kill him. He nursed his anger by keeping a list of Sobo's behavior recorded in a small notebook left over from school. The lines he recorded most were *Sobo likes Neliya. This morning Sobo talked to Neliya when she carried water from the well. Today Sobo's eyes followed Neliya all day. Neliya doesn't like Sobo. She is only showing off. Sobo is an evil man. He is an ugly hyena.*

Joseph fantasized about going to the city to buy a gun. He imagined meeting Sobo in the bush, pointing the gun at his face, and ordering him to stay away from Neliya before shooting him. If he killed Sobo with a phwitika, he would have to sneak into Alick's kitchen hut at night to chop off his head, but that might get Alick into trouble with the local police or the spirits of his matrilineal kin. He thought about using magic from the medicine his grandfather had taught him before his death, but he might be killed or banned from the village if the people suspected he used magic. Besides, he was not sure he had sufficient skill to make his medicine strong enough for a hyena like Sobo. He thought about all the terrible things he could do to Sobo, but in more rational moments, he knew he couldn't kill Sobo; he only wanted to make him go away. He was afraid, and ashamed to let Kakalulu know his dark thoughts.

One morning while Kakalulu was running an errand for his uncle, and Sobo was bathing at the river, Joseph saw Mwanda standing alone pounding maize in a mortar outside her kitchen. He approached and stood at a polite distance waiting to be recognized. He watched the muscles in her thin arms and shoulders contract and relax as she lifted the heavy pole and thrust it into the mortar. He listened to the hollow boom of the pounding, the rhythmic chant which escaped from her lips as she sang to make her work easier, and the familiar popping sounds exploding from her diaphragm each time the pole crushed grain. Her soiled headcloth, tied in back and smooth against her forehead, accentuated the wrinkles on her face. Only her eyes recognized his presence.

"*Sikomo*," she said, giving him permission to speak. "What's troubling you?"

"*Sikomo*," he answered. "You work too hard. The visitor is always hungry."

"Eh-h-h-h-," she agreed, with a musical utterance low in her throat.

"I need your advice, mother," His voice was almost a whisper. "What is the proper way to rid the village of the hyena?"

She turned away, her gaze resting on the maize inside the mortar. For a moment he thought she hadn't heard. When she spoke, her voice was also a whisper."We must find a way."

"I have thought of using the medicine my grandfather taught me, but I'm afraid."

"Don't be afraid. You would do the village a great service." Her shoulders sagged with fatigue, and for the first time, Joseph noticed how old and frail she was.

"I am afraid my medicine isn't strong enough for such a hyena."

Mwanda's eyes surveyed the village before she whispered, "I will help you, but he may yet prove to be my husband's cousin. He must not die."

"I only want to send him away."

"Tomorrow you will go to Kagolo, my home village, to see Kasinda. He knows the magic of *mankhwala*."

"Will he give me medicine?"

"He will tell you what to do. You must go when nobody is watching. Meet me at noon on the path to the well. I will give you a chicken to take for payment."

"Will you give me a sign for our meeting?"

"When you hear me coughing, come into the bush. Wait beside the baobab tree near the termite hill." Mwanda bent over the mortar pretending to examine the crushed maize; she let the coarse pieces sift through her fingers. "Nobody must discover our secret."

"My lips are sealed, mother."

"Tell Kasinda I sent you. He's my cousin."

"*Sikomo*," Joseph said, placing his hands together in respect.

Then in a voice so loud that other women in the village might hear, Mwanda scolded, "You're a bad influence. You must not keep me from my work."

When Joseph arrived at Kagolo village, it was almost dark. He had walked a long way carrying the live chicken under his arm, its legs hobbled with strips of bark. He found Kasinda sitting on a stool outside the door of his hut. Kasinda was an old man. His hair was gray; the Ngoni tribal marks were deep on skin tough and creased like rhinoceros hide. The lobes of his pierced ears sagged with the weight of large wooden pegs filling the holes. He was dressed in ragged walking shorts, his chest was bare, and his voice trembled from the chill of on-coming night.

"I am expecting you," Kasinda said.

Joseph clapped his hands in greeting. He was not surprised that Kasinda knew he was coming; diviners can know everything.

"I came to see you on a matter of great importance," Joseph said. "I was sent by Mwanda."

The old man led Joseph inside his hut where they sat cross-legged on a raffia mat on the dirt floor. A kerosene lantern in one corner of the square hut provided a pale light. The air in the windowless room was alive with a rare combination of fragrant medicinal herbs mingled with the acrid aroma of mold and decay. Bottles and tin cans filled with powders, crushed leaves, and wet fermenting potions sat in clusters on wooden shelves, and bunches of herbs, dried bark, animal skins, and bone hung from the eaves. Charred medicines lay in patches on large dried leaves. A basket beside Kasinda held his divining tools, including bowls, bones, tortoise shells, a small antelope horn, and a rattling gourd. Joseph placed the chicken on the mat and waited.

Kasinda lifted a shallow bowl fired of dark clay from the basket beside him. He poured water into the bowl and chanted, moving his hand in a circle above the bowl, his cracked voice rising and falling in rhythmic tones. Joseph's eyes grew heavy, his body limp, his mind flowed with the rhythm. When his head felt light and his body swayed to the pull of an ancient voice,

Kasinda said to Joseph, "Look into the water. Do you see what's troubling you?"

Joseph bent over the bowl. In dim light, he saw a distorted reflection staring back at him. "Yes, that's Sobo!" he cried. "That's the hyena who came uninvited to our village! He says he's the headman's cousin, but I don't believe him."

Kasinda moved the bowl of water to one side and took a black gourd from his divining basket. His thin fingers poured powdered medicine inside the gourd and rubbed the outside with oil. He shook the gourd, passed it around his head three times, and stood it upright on the dirt floor of the hut. He told Joseph to watch it and clap his hands in respect for the spirit inside. Joseph stared so intently at the gourd he didn't see Kasinda's lips move when he spoke.

"*A Mai*," Kasinda said, addressing the gourd as mother. "Please help us. Tell us what you know of this man, Sobo."

Wheezing sounds resonated through the hut and faded like a dying spirit to a faint whistle. Kasinda turned his head to one side, listening with his good ear.

"You are quite right," he said to Joseph. "Sobo has no relatives in your village."

"Who sent him?" Joseph asked.

The garbled tones of the gourd filled the hut again.

"She said your dead uncle sent him. Your mother's elder brother sent Sobo to test your power. You must get rid of him or great harm will come to you and your village."

"But how can I do that? I'm young and the elders don't listen to me."

"You heard Joseph," Kasinda said, addressing the gourd. "What can you tell him?"

The gourd made muffled cackling sounds.

"Oh, no, *A mai*," Kasinda politely disagreed. "That medicine is not strong enough."

The gourd wheezed.

"I beg your forgiveness," Kasinda said. "I don't know where to get the medicine you suggest. Please advise a medicine I can provide."

The gourd wheezed and whistled again while Kasinda bent over it listening again with his good ear.

"Yes, I think that would be satisfactory. Thank you, *A Mai*. I'll explain to Joseph. Sikomo." He clapped his hands and returned the gourd to the basket.

"She said to give you white medicine to make a line on the ground in front of the door of Sobo's sleeping hut," Kasinda explained. "When Sobo passes over the line, he will get sick and he might die.

"I don't want him to die," Joseph protested. "I only want him to leave the village."

Kasinda shook his head. "We don't always have control over the power of medicine."

With a small gourd, Kasinda dipped white powder into a brown paper bag and gave it to Joseph. "Take care you don't get the medicine on your hands when you pour it on the ground. This medicine has strong magic."

Joseph took the bag and waited while Kasinda rummaged through a wooden box holding small packages tied with string. He held one against the light of the lantern, squinting with one eye. Handing it to Joseph, he said, "Take this to my cousin, Mwanda. She will know what to do."

On the way home, Joseph fingered the small package trying to guess what was inside. He wouldn't think of opening it, but he felt for lumps, textures, shapes. He pressed the package to his nose, recognizing the odor of leaves from the poison plant used in "trial-by-poisoning" and smiled. He remembered stories about the old days. When a crime or theft was committed in the village, elders fed adults the poison plant and sent them to the river to drink water. The person who died was guilty.

Joseph was standing among the crowd the morning Sobo awoke to the clamor of voices outside his hut. Sobo pulled the grass door aside and peered out.

"What is troubling you?" he called.

Mwanda pointed to the white powder stretching in a straight line on the packed clay in front of his door. The wrinkles in outer corners of her eyes crinkled into small birds' tracks.

"Somebody is trying to bewitch you," she said.

Joseph saw fear pass like a shadow over Sobo's face; his hands moved involuntarily to his forehead before he regained composure. Sobo folded his arms across his chest and smiled.

"I was educated at a mission school in Lusaka. I don't believe in bewitching."

The crowd stared in disbelief, their faces sober, angry, accusing.

Joseph knew Sobo was frightened but listened, fascinated, as he turned clever phrases trying to change the minds of the people.

"Isn't this Mwanda's kitchen?" he asked, smiling.

Mwanda agreed that it was.

Sobo shrugged. "Then somebody must be trying to bewitch Mwanda." Uncertain eyes turned from Sobo to Mwanda and back to Sobo. For a moment, he looked triumphant.

"This medicine was not intended for me," he said, spreading his arms wide. "Look. Nothing will happen."

Sobo stepped defiantly over the line of white powder.

The crowd backed away, gasping.

Then folding his arms across his chest, Sobo stood with his chin high as people drifted away in two's and threes's. Women disappeared into huts; men stood in small groups at the edge of the village talking in low tones.

Joseph lingered, watching Sobo. Then he strolled to the boys' hut in the center of the village where he sat on the wooden stool outside the door. From there, he watched Mwanda kneel to serve Sobo breakfast porridge, her eyes downcast, her face without expression.

Later, he heard Sobo complain of thirst and stomach pains but pretended not to watch as he drank with great thirst from a clay pot filled with water. When Sobo rushed into the bush, stopping every few steps to vomit, Joseph and Kakalulu were busy mending a bamboo fishing trap. They looked at each other and smiled, knowing when Sobo recovered from vomiting, he would move on to another village.

Nobody was surprised when Sobo didn't return to Kadende. They said he was crazy to show disrespect for *ufiti*. When men sat at night in front of Alick's house drinking beer, they repeated their complaints and told other stories of how the spirits punish people who fail to follow the customs of ancestors. Women laughed and told stories of Sobo's attempts to seduce them, agreeing that Sobo was a fool. Joseph and Mwanda listened to the stories with a solemn faces, guarding their secret.

Joseph counted the paper money hidden in a tin can in his hut and decided the time had come. He went to his uncle Sitifana's hut to speak to him in private. "It is time for me to take a wife," he said, "and I have chosen Neliya." Sitifana stood on one foot and then the other, making a small rocking motion.

"Will you arrange with Headman Kadende and Mwanda for a meeting?"

"Eh-h-h," he said at last. "That's not possible."

"Why not?" Joseph's words were more a sob than a question.

"Kakalulu and his uncles are meeting with them on Sunday. Didn't he tell you his plans?"

Joseph shook his head. He wanted to cry out that his best friend and age-mate had betrayed him, but he didn't want to lose composure in his uncle's presence. He was sure Kakalulu knew how he felt about Neliya. He knew Kakalulu must have suspected what he was going to do. He may have read his notebook.

Joseph put both hands to his face to hide the pain. He turned away, ashamed for his uncle to see his disappointment. He had worked so hard to get Sobo out of the village, he did not intend to give up easily.

"Will you speak to the Headman before Sunday?" Joseph asked. "Neliya should have some say in the decision."

"That is not possible." his uncle said. "We must not interfere or go against tradition. We might make enemies and someone would bewitch us."

"I thought it was always understood that Neliya would be my wife," he insisted.

Sitifana was getting impatient with his nephew. "The strange ideas you picked up at that mission school have spoiled you," he said, his voice harsh.

Joseph thanked his uncle and walked away. He had helped Mwanda get rid of Sobo; perhaps Mwanda would do a favor for him. She could find some fault with Kakalulu and speak in Joseph's behalf. He was determined to find a way to speak to her alone.

He knew the Headman was old and easily swayed. Joseph thought about what he would do if the Headman promised Neliya to Kakalulu. In that case, he would have no reason to stay in the village. He knew he couldn't watch the girl he had always loved give birth to Kakalulu's children. He would try to be patient until Sunday. If Mwanda or Neliya had not spoken in his favor by then, he would walk to the Mission Station to talk with the priests about a scholarship to continue his education. He must control his feelings; it would be wrong to cause trouble for Sitifana. A restlessness swept over him. He remembered pictures of cities, countries, and distant places in his school books that remained with him like a dream. If he could not find contentment here, he would go away.

Lessons for Women

Anwelo awoke to the erratic chirping of birds. He lay on his side on the raffia mat on the floor of the small round hut, his face toward the door, his eyes staring into gray dawn. He was amazed at the panoramic view of the village through his open door, a village not yet awake. Panic seized him. He must see his Uncle Mtele at once. He dressed and rushed across the compound.

"*Hodi? Hodi?*" he called in a tremulous voice.

Mtele recognized the rich low tones of his nephew and stirred on his bed. "Aiee," he responded almost inaudibly, indicating he had heard.

He slipped into plastic thongs, drew over his head a ragged T-shirt which hung loose above his khaki shorts and opened the grass door, closing it behind him.

He watched Anwelo pace with quick, nervous movements, breathing heavily, nostrils dilating. He decided Anwelo needed time to choose his words before giving him permission to speak. He studied Anwelo's smooth ebony skin, his large black eyes shaded by long lashes, and his strong masculine shoulders. His good looks made him too attractive to women, and Mtele had feared for some time that somebody would be jealous and place a curse upon him.

"Tell me what is troubling you," he said at last.

"I must be very careful in this village," Anwelo said, clasping his hands behind his back. He wanted to say everything at once, but he knew he must show respect for his uncle by speaking with caution.

"Are you unhappy here?" Mtele asked after another long silence.

Anwelo's words came tumbling over each other in spite of his efforts at restraint. "There are big women in this village," he said. "They are very dangerous."

"Eh-h-h-," Mtele agreed. "There are older women without husbands. They can be dangerous."

"People say Cimutu village has a reputation for witchcraft," Anwelo continued, still agitated. "I must be careful."

"Has somebody tried to bewitch you?" Mtele's eyes looked past Anwelo to the cluster of huts behind him where the widows of the village had built their houses. His eyes rested for a moment on Sonile's hut. Her third husband had recently died, and the headman suspected she had killed him with her magic.

"Before I went to sleep last night, I closed the door of my hut and fastened it," Anwelo said. "This morning the door was open and I could see the entire village." His eyes grew large with fear; he searched his uncle's face for assurance that something would be done.

"Did you forget to close the door last night?" Mtele asked, hoping Anwelo might have had a lapse of memory.

"Oh no," Anwelo insisted. "I would never forget anything so important."

"Have you quarreled with somebody?" Mtele probed, trying to uncover the reason for threats to Anwelo's safety.

"No," Anwelo said, "but somebody opened my door last night and was sitting outside watching me sleep. Somebody is trying to bewitch me."

"Who would do this thing?" Mtele mused. He scratched his matted hair with a crooked forefinger trying to recall any strange behavior he might have noticed among the villagers.

"I don't know, "Anwelo said, "but Sonile has been giving me dark looks. When I see her, she smiles, but when she thinks I'm not looking, her face is dark and angry.

Mtele nodded in agreement. "She is a bad woman." After a moment, he added, "And she has a bewitched toe."

From a distance, Sonile looked like other women in the village. Her modest cotton dress which hung to her ankles camouflaged a muscular but shapely figure. Her head cloth, flat against her forehead and tied in a knot at the back of her neck, emphasized high cheek bones and vaguely oriental eyes. Also, like other women in the village, she was always barefoot, but on her right foot, the little toe was round, red, and bulbous, swollen to the fullness of ripe passion fruit. Since the mysterious death of her third husband with stomach pains, she had lived alone with her son, Malilo, a small sullen boy who looked like his mother.

"I will not sleep in that hut again." Anwelo regretted sounding so ungrateful. He meant no disrespect to his uncle, but fear made him rash.

Mtele studied the ground embarrassed by Anwelo's harsh words. He pursed his lips and said, "You can sleep in my kitchen hut, or you can ask the headman's permission to sleep in the boys' hut."

"I will sleep in your kitchen," Anwelo said. "I'm too old to sleep with boys. I'm a working man."

"You are a working man," Mtele said, "but you don't have money for a bride. Until that time, as your mother's eldest brother, you are my responsibility."

Anwelo lowered his eyes. He knew Mtele intended to remind him that although he had just graduated from secondary school, he must show proper respect. His job at the Tsetse Fly Control Gate paid more than most farmers in Cimutu village earned, and soon he would have enough saved to have a wife to cook for him. In the meantime, he must remember to give his uncle more money.

The morning sun had washed the village in a golden glow by the time Anwelo had gathered his clothes and his school books and tied them in his blanket. As he left the hut, he was startled to see Sonile standing a few feet from his door. She made it obvious she was there to watch. He stopped suddenly when their eyes met.

Sonile's face broke into a wide toothy grin which revolted him, inciting a cold trickle down his spine.

As he continued across the compound carrying his heavy bundle under one arm and his sleeping mat under the other, he glanced back. He was shocked to see her lips fixed in mirthless undefined mockery and her eyes smoldering with a fire that might have been hatred.

His uncle stood at the kitchen door to receive him and supervise the arrangement of his things. "When I see big women," Anwelo said, "I feel my fingers getting long and thin." Mtele nodded, understanding his fear.

On the third day after Anwelo moved into his uncle's kitchen, he came home from work to see Sonile walking toward him from the direction of her little house. She carried in her arms a small clay pot of *nsima* covered with a circular crocheted cloth; bright red beads dangled from the edges. He tried to ignore her.

"I brought a gift," she said.

Anwelo pretended not to hear.

"I will cook *nsima* for you."

Anwelo was shocked. Her proposition suggested marriage, the kind of marriage not recognized by custom. He was too embarrassed to look at her face with its wicked smile, but if he looked at her feet, he might see her bewitched toe. He averted his face and stared at the ground.

"I do not wish to trouble you, *A Mai*," he said softly, calling her "mother" as a term of respect and to let her know he considered her an older woman. "My uncle's third wife, Balila, cooks for me." Balila was young and pretty, and he thought mentioning her name might send Sonile a message to mind her own business. He went inside and closed the door.

There was nothing for Sonile to do but go away.

The next evening Sonile brought firewood which she put beside the door; his uncle advised his wives not to touch the wood as it might contain magic. On the following evening, Sonile brought boiled yams which Anwelo also refused. Then on the fourth day, Sonile surprised everyone by staying inside her hut all day. That night someone sent owls to dance upon the roof while Anwelo slept.

"*Muphe! Muphe! Nimkukute!*" (Kill him! Kill him! That I may eat him) the owls shrieked as they scratched and danced on the thatched roof above Anwelo's head. He felt beads of sweat pop out on his forehead and lay trembling throughout the night. At daybreak, the owls went away. Anwelo dressed and ran to seek the advice of his uncle.

"*Hodi? Hodi?*" he called outside his uncle's hut.

"What is it now?" Mtele grumbled, sticking his head out the door. He had been up late the night before drinking maize beer with friends. He was in no mood to be disturbed.

"I must leave this village at once," Anwelo said, wringing his hands.

"Why must you go in such a hurry?"

"Somebody is bewitching me!"

"What happened this time?"

"Sonile sent owls to dance on my roof, calling "'*Muphe! Muphe, nimkukute!*'"

Mtele's eyes opened wide. "This is serious. We must see the headman at once."

Headman Cimutu met with Mtele and Anwelo under the big tree beside his mud-brick house as was his custom when problems needed to be solved. Three tawny dogs sniffed the ground hungrily at their feet while they talked. As Anwelo told his story, the headman listened. He nodded in recognition when Mtele interrupted to embellish Anwelo's story with "facts" of his own.

"This is definitely a case for a diviner," Mtele said forcefully. "There is no other way to know if Sonile is guilty."

He watched the headman's reaction. He knew the headman had been educated in a missionary school and consulted diviners only when there was nothing else to be done. Some jealous people who opposed the headman whispered that he made decisions "too much like Europeans."

Headman Cimutu sat with a dreamy look in his eyes and rubbed the stubble on his chin before answering. "Perhaps," he said, "you are right, but I have a plan." The wooden chair creaked as he leaned his broad shoulders against it and rubbed his chest while he gazed at the sky. "Anwelo," he said, "you must help us. You must do exactly as I say."

Two days later, Anwelo went to Sonile's hut. She sat on the ground with one foot tucked under her and the leg with the bewitched toe extended. Two mounds of sloppy clay lay beside her, a large one of light red ocher and a smaller on of dark umber. She was turning a pot in the bottom of an enameled basin. Sonile rotated the basin, shaping the clay skillfully with her big hands.

"*Sikomo*," Anwelo greeted her, his voice almost a whisper.

Sonile pretended to ignore him while she rounded the sides with a corn cob and smoothed them with a piece of broken shell.

Anwelo was impressed with her skill, but he hated her for showing her power by refusing to acknowledge his presence.

"Do you want me to make a pot for you?" Sonile asked after she had made him wait long enough to feel humiliated.

"You make fine pots," Anwelo said. "You should sell that one at the market. It will bring a good price."

Sonile's petulance changed to undisguised pleasure. The sour droop of her mouth turned upward into a wide grin exaggerating her large front teeth. When Anwelo said nothing more, she looked at him expectantly, questioning with her eyes.

"I need somebody to cook for me," he said.

"And what is wrong with Balila's cooking?" Sonile asked, her slanting eyes narrowed with suspicion. She was still smarting from his previous refusals. "Has her *nsima* no salt?"

"She refuses to cook for me," Anwelo said. "She says my uncle is making her do more than her share of work."

Sonile laughed an ugly mirthless laugh.

"What I am telling you is true," Anwelo said, "but it is all right if you are no longer interested." He turned his face away pretending he considered the matter closed.

Sonile shaped the narrow neck of the pot deftly with her long fingers and looked at him out of the corners of her eyes, her face still turned toward her work. "Do you think I will cook for you for nothing?" she hissed, and the corners of her mouth turned down again.

Anwelo had been coached by Headman Cimutu and Mtele; he was prepared for her comment. "Of course not. I'm a working man. Tell me your price."

Sonile laughed again. "That will depend upon how clever you are. Come to my house tonight when Malilo is asleep, and we will talk about the price."

When Anwelo realized the import of her words, he felt sick. He tried to look at her and smile, but what he felt was disgust and fear. She was an old woman with no shyness like the young girls his own age, and he was afraid of her bewitched toe.

"Let me sample your cooking first," he said. "If you make *nsima* with relish as well as you make pots, I will pay a good price, but tonight would not be a good night."

She laughed again, but this time the laughter sounded real. Anwelo knew she thought he had not understood her offer.

"I will cook for you tomorrow," she said, "and then we shall see."

When he finally said "*Sikomo*," and walked away, he was exhausted.

He cast a backward glance and was shocked by the viciousness distorting Sonile's face, but the instant she saw him turn, she replaced the expression with sweetness. He wondered if he had been clever enough to do what the headman had asked of him.

Next morning, while Anwelo was washing his hands and face in a basin outside the kitchen, Sonile brought *nsima*. She knelt respectfully and placed the pot beside the door, displaying her toothy smile. Anwelo took the food inside his hut, but when Sonile was out of sight, he carried it to the headman's house.

Late that afternoon, the headman sent a messenger around the village ordering everyone to meet at once beneath the big tree beside his house. People grumbled that the short notice was interfering with their work, but they were really disgruntled that the notice was too sudden for them to find out what the meeting would be about.

When Anwelo arrived, the women were already sitting on the ground in a cluster on one side of the big tree; the men sat in a group on the other. Holding a staff in his right hand, topped by a brass knob, the headman sat at a wooden table. He had arranged the chairs in a semicircle for the elders. Anwelo knew something important was about to happen.

Usually, the headman opened such meetings with praise for the elders who helped him make decisions, and he almost always made a long speech reviewing the history and background of the issue to be decided. This day was different; he called the elders to take their places and stood before the silent crowd.

"Sonile will come forward," he called.

Sonile looked startled, but after recovering from her surprise, she walked to the table and stood proud and defiant, her chin held high, her back straight. Anwelo was sure he could see nervousness in her eyes and in the movements of her hands.

"State your name," the headman said. He used the white man's method of conducting meetings which sometimes made village people uncomfortable. They tolerated his methods because his decisions were fair and wise and still in keeping with Chewa customs.

"Sonile Phili."

"That was your last husband's name. Tell us your real name."

"From which husband?"

"How many husbands have you had?"

"I can't remember exactly. Two. Maybe five. I think it might be seven."

"When were you first married?"

"That depends upon which marriage you are talking about."

The village people sat in silence, their eyes wide with shock. They couldn't imagine anyone, especially a woman, talking to the headman in such a rude and arrogant manner.

"She must be crazy," an old woman whispered.

"Beat her! Beat her!" a chorus of men called. The headman held up his staff to quiet them.

"Where is your first husband living?" the headman asked, emphasizing the word "first."

"Husbands are not dependable," Sonile sneered. "He is not here."

"Is he living or dead?"

"He might be dead. No, I think he might be living."

"She is hiding," the elder sitting to the right of Headman Cimutu murmured in disgust.

"He divorced you, didn't he?" The headman intended to make a case out of her failure as a wife.

"He is one of the lost ones. Sonile said. The hard edge of her voice softened. "He went away to work in Bulawayo and did not return."

"He went away because you were trying to bewitch him with your magic. Is that not true?"

"I do not know magic," Sonile said. "I know only good medicine."

"People say you are a witch," the headman said, baiting her to lose her composure.

"People lie!" Sonile cried. "People are jealous because I sell pots, and I can buy my own dresses. I do not need a husband."

"What caused the death of your second husband?" the headman asked, ignoring her outburst.

"He had a pain in the chest."

"Did you bewitch him?"

"He had a pain in his chest," she repeated.

"What caused the death of your third husband?"

"A pain in the stomach." Sonile's eyes narrowed with anger and rebellion. She knew the headman was trying to trick her. Her deceased husband was the headman's cousin, Jacob Phili. The headman had been present at the funeral. The headman had supervised the *cale* ritual of placing unfinished beer in a shrine at the foot of the *nsolo* tree as an offering to the spirits. He had assigned people to sit by the grave to prevent *mphelanjilu* from digging up the body and consuming the corpse. He knew everything. Why was he asking her these questions?

"Did you bewitch him?" the headman asked, his face as inscrutable as stone.

"I do not know who bewitched him," Sonile said evenly. "He died of a pain in the stomach."

"Did you kill him with your poison?"

"I know nothing of poison," Sonile said, but Anwelo noticed Sonile was beginning to tremble.

"Is it true you offered to cook for Anwelo Phili?" the headman asked.

Some of the older women gasped, shocked that Sonile had no shame.

"Yes, but he refused," she said, sounding annoyed.

"He later accepted your offer, did he not?"

"Yes."

"And you tried to poison him with your magic."

"You lie!" Sonile screamed.

Gasps of shock and reproach resonated from the audience. Everyone knew the decision would go against her. Chewa courts aim at removing hatred in the hearts of men and women, but this woman's anger was proof of her wickedness.

Sonile pointed to Anwelo sitting at the edge of the group of men. "He sits there looking fat and healthy," she challenged. "How can you say I poisoned him?"

The headman tapped the table with his staff. Two men who had been hiding in the headman's house came out carrying the body of the headman's dog on a mat. They placed it in front of Sonile.

"This is the evidence," the headman said. "You cooked

nsima and relish for Anwelo which he did not eat. We fed it to this dog. He had pains in the stomach and died. What can you say for yourself? You cannot deny you intended to poison Anwelo with powerful magic."

"He deserved it!" Sonile screamed.

"Why?" the headman asked gently. "Anwelo has not troubled you."

"He is a man!" Sonile cried. "Men beat women. Men make women carry everything from the fields. Men drink beer while women pound maize and hoe in gardens . . ." Her muscles trembled, her face contorted, she frothed at the mouth as she continued to report her grievances against men. It was as if a lifetime of pain and disappointment exploded from her taut and tortured body.

Village men howled and cried out in protest.

"She is a witch!"

"She is crazy!"

"Beat her to make her obedient!"

Headman Cimutu stood tall, holding his staff in both hands, its polished brass knob reflected the golden light of the late afternoon sun.

"The elders and I have decided that Sonile must leave this place at once and go to another village," he said, "if she can find a village that will take her."

The crowd was silent, staring at Sonile with mixed emotions. They knew having no village was worse than death. She would be a beggar, a wanderer, despised and suspected by everyone who met her. All eyes turned to Malilo standing wide-eyed and frightened beside the men.

"And she will take Malilo with her," he added. "He has no relatives in this village."

When the meeting adjourned, men stood in ragged groups

shaking their heads, clucking their tongues, talking among themselves in low tones.

Women slunk, bewildered and humiliated, into their huts, fearing their husbands might beat them for Sonile's arrogance and disrespect.

A young woman nursing an infant walked among them with a puzzled frown. "Maybe Sonile is right," she murmured. Old women quieted her with small hissing sounds; they feared for her safety. They spoke out in voices loud enough for the men to hear:

"Sonile is a dangerous woman."

"She has no respect for the elders."

"It is our duty to carry maize from the fields."

"It is right for a man to beat a disobedient wife."

Sonile tied her meager possessions in a blanket and left the village at sundown. Holding Malilo by the hand, she walked through the bush in the direction of her field hut where she would probably spend the night before moving on. Women gathered to watch her go, puzzled by her mocking smile and derisive laughter. But they were not surprised when next day nothing was left of her evil spirit but a pile of ashes where her hut had been.

Celebration

Women of Gombe Village clustered in a half-circle around the bonfire built to celebrate the night of a full moon when it was light enough to dance and watched the fast-moving feet of dancers. Men gathered in a ragged group opposite, completing the circle. Behind them, mud and thatch huts spread like dark shadows in gray gloom of moonlight.

Vida stood near the fire holding her baby wrapped in a length of faded blue cloth. The child looked thin and spidery and younger than five month because Vida's breast milk was drying and the infant was weak and hungry. Vida wore no head cloth like other women. The dust settling on her close-cropped hair dulled its natural gloss and emphasized large sad eyes and a full mouth in a childlike face. Josiyele, her husband, stood facing her on the other side of the flames. Firelight illuminated his khaki shorts, striped T-shirt, vacant smile, and glazed eyes. With both hands, he held himself in the crotch like an excited little boy—and giggled. People crowding around pretended not to notice, but Vida glanced at him from time to time, looked embarrassed, and tried to smile.

Singing guitars, talking drums, excited cries, and fast-dancing feet created a happy mood. Children danced alone in the center, circling the fire, hips twisting, feet flying, raising clouds of yellow dust. Young men and women danced self-consciously on the outer fringes of the circle at the edge of darkness. An old crone called, "Chewa women are shy during the day, but they are brave at night," and clapped her hands for three girls dancing together, twisting sideways into the circle, gyrating around the fire. Flickering light focused on fast-moving legs and bare feet. Dust clouds rose from stamping feet as dancers writhed to rapid beating of the drums and strumming of guitars. Children sat on the ground to watch; old people called out names of relatives to sing and dance.

Kenala, a skinny, bare-chested teenager wearing an athletic whistle around his neck, assigned himself master of ceremonies. He held a scrap of yellowed paper in his hand, calling out names, assembling dance groups to match the mood.

"Ladies and gentlemen," he called, raising his hands high. "We will now see dancing by Sofiya, Etelina, and Tiyesko." He bowed low and withdrew as the girls moved inside the circle. Drumbeats accelerated to a frenzy, guitars wailed, hands clapped. Old women ululated, their tongues thudding vibrant, yodeling sounds. The audience chanted, cheered, faces aglow, eyes fastened to twirling bodies, flicking feet, gyrating hips. The rapid music, throbbing drums, and bouncing breasts of dancing girls monitored heartbeats of old men, arousing young passions.

Kenala lifted the athletic whistle to his lips, blowing a shrill note to get attention. The music stopped and part of the magic was lost to visions of settling dust, the sounds of dancers panting from exhaustion, and a burst of ululating. A tremulous cry arose among the men.

"Now we will have dancing by men," Kenala called, moving momentarily into firelight. A tall thin man pounded a syncopated rhythm on his drum. Two guitars wailed as young men drifted into the circle of light. The pace of the music increased; agile bodies responded to the talking drum.

Josiyele did not join the dancers but tried to make his way

unnoticed to his hut. Vida's eyes followed his path as he dissolved into night. Hugging the baby close, she edged her way through the crowd and followed, her bare feel silent in thick dust. She opened the grass door, slipping silently inside. Light from the kerosene lantern on a small wooden table outlined Josiyele's slender figure, casting a long shadow on the wall behind him. He turned suddenly. It was as she suspected. He held wrapping papers for smoking in one hand and a small bag in the other. He was smoking *cambia* again. She trembled. There would be more beatings.

"Please," she begged, her voice barely audible above the throbbing of the music."You must not smoke *cambia*."

He sneered. His eyes were bloodshot and dropped as they always did when he had been smoking. "It is proper for a man to give orders to a woman," he said, "not a woman to a man."

She knew it was dangerous to speak strong words to a husband. She had been told many times the story of Sonile and what happened to women who did not show proper respect for men, but the night and the music made her brave.

"You are not Josiyele when you smoke," she said. "You have no reason. You fight with people."

She dared not mention the beatings he gave her when he was not himself.

His lips curled with contempt. "You lie. I know what I do."

"Sometimes you are like a wild man," she said. "One day you may kill, and the police will come to take you away."

"I have no worries when I smoke," Josiyele said, rolling the crushed hemp into the soiled paper. "You are a bad wife; you do not want me to feel good."

Vida watched him with sad eyes. He had not smoked before he went away to work at the Copperbelt. When his work was finished, he came home a different husband. He was cruel to her, and he was disrespectful to his elders. If he could only find work! She watched him hold the homemade cigarette between his thumb and finger and blow foul-smelling smoke into the tiny room.

"You will go home to your village," he said. "You are not a good wife."

Vida was silent. He always told her to go home when he had been smoking, and sometimes he beat her to make her go. But she stayed. She couldn't believe he really wanted her to go away; he and his fathers had paid many *kwachas* to her parents for the bride's price. Always, the morning after the beatings, he did not seem to remember what he had said or done.

Vida knew she had been a good wife. She had done all the things her grandmothers had taught her when it was time to "give words" at the *cinemwali* ceremony. They had told her to go into the bush, gather firewood, bring it back, make a fire, draw water and warm the water for washing her husband's legs. They had told her to heat water in a clay pot, pour the maize meal for making nsima, stir it until it was smooth, add more maize meal, put in a dash of water, kneel when she served her husband, and serve him unsalted nsima on the first day of her bleeding so he would know she was unclean. They had told her word upon word how to go to the bush to pick wild greens, how to hoe and plant vegetables, and how she must carry the harvest from the fields. They had given many words about how to smear mud on the walls of her hut, and how to cut and carry long grass for thatching the roof. They had taught her erotic dances and had told her in exact words how to arouse and satisfy her husband—and all the things she must do to be obedient. They had struck her and caned her to prove that she was strong at heart and would not embarrass her husband by crying out when he beat her. She had been able to do all those things her grandmothers had taught her. How could he say she was not a good wife? Vida felt useless in his presence knowing he could not reason. She put her hands to her face; tears dripped between her fingers, but Josiyele's heart was hard.

"I have a girl friend," he said. "I will take her as my second wife. If that does not please you, then you will go home to your village."

Vida believed he was saying these things to torture her. Only old men in her village took second or third wives. When brothers died, it was their duty to marry the widow and take the children so they would not go hungry. That she could accept, but Josiyele had no work. How could he pay for another wife? Where would she live? Her eyes surveyed the walls of the tiny hut he had built for her. She had collected clay of different colors, made designs on the walls, made it beautiful.

Her eyes moved to a place on the earth floor beneath the small wooden table where the flame of the lantern flickered. Josiyele had built the table for her when they were married, and on their wedding night, they had cut pubic hairs and buried them together in that special place under the table. She was already betrothed to Josiyele when she was given words at her *cinemwali*, and Josiyele himself had taken away her coldness, not a *fisi*, a ritual friend. Josiyele belonged to her; the house belonged to her, and she would have no other woman living in it.

Even in the dim light, she could see Josiyele's drooping eyelids, his red-rimmed eyes. He was not the Josiyele she had married. When he smoked, he was a stranger, a crazy man with no mind of his own. If he could not help himself, then she must help him. She would find a way. She placed the baby gently on the floor beside the table while she untied the sleeping mat from the eaves of the hut. She unrolled the mat on the floor, put the baby on it, and covered it with the strip of blue cloth. When she stood up to speak to Josiyele, he had vanished, gone back to the dancing and drums and the celebration of the full moon. She felt ashamed. She knew people at Gombe Village avoided looking at him because they were ashamed also. He was disgracing himself in the eyes of his age group and in the eyes of the elders.

Vida searched the hut for bags of *cambia*. She looked through the clothes he kept in a wooden box, she felt with her fingertips around the eaves of the hut, but she found nothing. She looked for cracks in the walls where he might hide a small package, and she looked in storage pots. She found a bag in the baby's blanket which she had rolled up and hung from the ceiling to keep it clean and ready for cold weather in the dry season. She stood holding the package in her hands looking at it with hatred and disgust. *Cambia* was her enemy.

Josiyele burst through the door. "I was watching," he screamed. His face was as evil as the *nfiti*'s magic, and his fingers were long and thin as he reached for her. He threw her against the table. She fell to the floor. He bent over her, slapping her face, beating her shoulders with his clenched fists. Vida held her breath to keep from crying out, but the music was too loud for anyone to hear her cries. She groaned through clenched teeth. Josiyele's hands were at her throat, squeezing with the strength of a madman. He pressed her head against the floor and held it there, his hands still at her throat. Vida kicked violently. He slapped her again and again, first on one side of her face and then on the other. Vida lay limp and still. Josiyele shook her. When she did not respond, he stood up, looking down at her.

Outside the drums pounded their frenzied rhythms, raging, throbbing to the cries of the dancers, to the sounds of ululating, to the clapping of hands, to the raw mood of night. Josiyele stood over Vida with clenched fists. Then his fingers relaxed. He slumped, dazed and weary, frowning slightly as if groping for some fleeting thought, as if trying to get straight in his mind what he had done to the wife he loved. The awful power of the music throbbed in his head, the violent beating of drums kept time with the rapid beating of his heart. The chants, rhythms, delirious cries of dancers, and the pull of the full moon were forces too strong for him to cast off in moonlight.

Josiyele squatted beside Vida. With trembling hands, he shook her, expecting her to open her eyes and speak. When she did not, he laughed, hysteria in his choked voice. Then the tears came. When his thighs began to ache, he lay down beside her on the dirt floor. Losing all sense of time, he drifted into reverie to erase the terrible truth of what he had done. He saw himself throwing Vida's beautiful body in the fast-moving river. He saw her rise out of mist and smile at him, and then the water carried her away to a place he did not know. He saw himself going to his mother's house the next day to say, "My wife, your daughter-in-law, is not here. Tell me what to do." Then the next day or the next, his parents would walk to Vida's village to speak to her parents. They would wait to be invited to a private place, and they would say at the proper moment, "Your daughter is not here. She has gone away. We want our money back."

Josiyele's mind began to clear. Somewhere in his tired brain, a small circle of light flickered through his confusion, and he knew things would not be the way he imagined. Tomorrow the police would come for him, or even worse, the headman would make him leave the village forever, with no relatives and no place to go.

At the baby's weak cry, Vida stirred, groaning softly. Josiyele studied her face, breathless. He wanted to say he was sorry, but he could not bring himself to apologize to a woman. He wanted to be a better husband, but she didn't understand; nobody understood how he felt—that jobs were scarce and life was hard for a man with little education. He waited until she opened her eyes and put a hand on her thigh. He murmured, "Tomorrow, I will go to the game park to look for work."

The Proposal

Lufeyo's feet felt light as he got off the bus at Kaunda Square. There was a certain spring to his walk, overt testimony to feelings of anticipation mounting inside him. He watched his feet kick up miniature dust storms as he hurried along the unpaved street thinking of his meeting with Chitaminji.

Almost every Friday night for more than a year he had gone to visit her in the little house her husband built for her before his death. Lufeyo looked forward to the good food she prepared for him. Afterwards, when they were both comfortable and content from much eating and love-making, they strolled down the road to Ndozi Tavern where they drank with friends until midnight or until fatigue drove them home to sleep. Always, when morning came, Chitaminji sent him away. He remembered with irritation the times she'd refused to let him move into the house with her.

Lufeyo had mixed feelings about Chitaminji. She was not exactly the kind of good-time girl a man abandoned after he grew tired of her. Although she was now a city woman, her behavior was still that of a country woman and a good Chewa. She was modest and gentle, and she still treated men and her elders with respect. On the other hand, she was not exactly the kind of woman he wanted to marry. Chitaminji was a village girl with only a primary education, while he, Lufeyo Banda, had completed secondary school. As soon as he got a steady job, he planned to take night courses at the University of Zambia where he might meet a girl with education and standing while he was furthering his own education. Better still, he hoped to marry a woman with money. At the moment, he saw money as the greatest restraint to his becoming a very important person.

In the meantime, Chitaminji was the ideal girlfriend for such a man to have. Not only did she not ask for gifts and pretty dresses, but she was also able to provide him with a little cash when he needed it most. She owned a stall at the market where she sold soap, cooking oil, bread, and vegetables in season. When business was slow, she made fresh beer. Being a good business woman, she often had many *ngwee* tucked away in jars and tin cans. Once, during National Independence Week, she collected so much paper money she opened an account at Barclay's Bank to keep it safe, but Chitaminji was reluctant to talk about that.

She had one extravagance which annoyed him for reasons he could not explain fully to himself: she played the Pick-A-Lot Lottery weekly. For as long as he had known her, buying a Pick-A-Lot ticket was like an obsession with her. She'd walk any distance to buy one. Sometimes when he wanted her to cook for him or make love, she had walked into town to buy another ticket. He'd scolded her more than once by telling her that playing the lottery was like throwing money into the river. Chitaminji refused to listen. She'd turn her face away pretending not to hear. In her quiet way, she could be a very difficult and determined woman.

When he came in sight of her house, his pace increased. He saw her outlined against the two banana trees in back of her house. She sat on the ground beside the cooking pot preparing his food as usual, but as he approached, he saw there was a difference. She sat straight and still and did not respond to his greeting. Without speaking again, he sat in the chair she had placed nearby for his comfort. For several minutes, they sat together in silence.

"You are sad today," he said. "Tell me what is troubling you. Perhaps I can help."

"We must talk," she said and poked at the charcoal fire with a small stick. "We must talk about the future."

"I have not thought much about the future," Lufeyo said, resisting the direction of the conversation.

"I must know," she said. "What are your plans?"

"Plans?"

"Do you plan to marry me?"

"We are as good as married already," Lufeyo said, trying to make his voice sound gentle and loving. "Isn't that sufficient for the present?"

"No," she said, but Lufeyo sensed a softening in her manner.

"No," she repeated. "I want to go to the *boma* and make it legal."

Lufeyo gasped. He was shocked by her directness.

"You are behaving improperly for a woman," he said. The sharp edge of reproach hardened his voice.

Chitaminji lowered her eyes and studied the hand lying limp in her lap. After a moment, she looked straight at him for the first time and watched his face as she spoke.

"We have both had one proper marriage," she said, "and we are no longer children. We do not need the elders to decide for us. Times are changing, Lufeyo, and we can change with them."

"I do not like this change you speak of," Lufeyo said, his voice harsh. "I do not like the kind of change that makes women act like men and men become women. No woman will tell me what to do. Not even you, Chitaminji."

"I must know," Chitaminji insisted. "I must know now. Is there someone else?"

Lufeyo felt anger rising like a whirlwind in the dry season carrying with it the dust of his confusion. He did not want to marry her, but he was not ready to give her up—not yet. He needed a woman, and he wanted that woman to be Chitaminji for the present. She was spoiling a perfectly good situation for him. Why did she have to be so difficult? Well, if she wanted the truth, he would give it to her.

"My plans for the future do not include any woman," he said, trying to keep his voice calm. "I want to get more education. I want to make a lot of money. Someday, I am going to be a very important person."

Chitaminji's shoulders sagged. She turned her face away from him and said, "That is a good thing for me to know."

She rose, straightened her chitinji cloth, tucked it in at the waist, and smoothed it over her hips.

"Then it is finished," she said.

She lifted the porcelain cooking pot from the fire by the long handle. Without looking at Lufeyo again, she carried the pot of curried stew into the house and shut the door leaving him outside. Lufeyo watched her go thinking he had never seen such a look on a woman's face. Was it disappointment? Anger?

"Foolish woman!" he fumed as he followed the road to Ndozi Tavern. "She could at least have waited until I'd taken her to bed."

He kicked a stone stirring up a small spray of dust and began to plan what he would do with his wasted evening. First, he would get drunk, and then he would find a girlfriend who did not want to talk of marriage. It was a good idea, anyway, not to spend too much time with one woman; they got the feeling after a while that they owned a man. How stupid it was of Chitaminji to try to force him into a decision.

Soon he stood at the bar with a bottle of beer in his hand. He was thinking that he always enjoyed the first beer most—the exciting stinging sensation as it went down, followed by a delicious warmth and numbness. His friend Tomo Zulu was already drunk. He greeted Lufeyo by throwing an unsteady arm around his shoulders.

"Congratulations," he said in a loud voice.

"For what?" Lufeyo asked, trying to pull away. He was in no mood for Tomo's familiarity.

"All these people are expecting you to buy drinks." Tomo swung his free arm in the direction of the room full of patrons.

"Why? What's the occasion?" Lufeyo asked, and he turned to look out upon a mass of expectant faces.

"You are the one with the rich girlfriend!" Tomo said, laughing.

"What do you mean?" asked an incredulous Lufeyo beginning to feel a twinge of panic.

"Stop teasing us," Tomo scolded. His words slurred and his body swayed as he spoke. "Everybody here knows Chitaminji is the Pick-A-Lot winner of two hundred thousand *kwacha*."

BATTLE OF THE BEES

When Charles accepted a scientific research job in East Africa for a year to study the mating habits of hyenas, Kay expected to make some household adjustments but wasn't prepared for what they would be. She felt the first impact of change when the African Studies Institute near Lusaka, Zambia assigned them to an old English house left over from days of Colonialism. It was a tall two-story brick building with a steep roof that hadn't been lived in for years.

Kay was delighted at first but soon found the huge kitchen, workroom, and dining room so vast and unworkable she took a three-mile hike each time she served a simple meal. Electricity was off most of the time, but the tiny English cooker made mealtime a challenge even when it was on. Washing machines were things of the future; she did laundry by hand in concrete tubs in the back yard. Eventually, they hired Abelo, a Chewa "houseboy" who was continually underfoot because Kay was not accustomed to dealing with servants.

The greatest cultural impact occurred with her sudden exposure to the variety of fauna which had taken possession of the house in the absence of human habitation. Tiny flesh-colored frogs with freckles and red feet plopped out of water faucets. Small lizards scurried about in vines on the outside walls and slithered into the house through an open door. Ants and roaches claimed the kitchen. Bush babies, small rodents with wide eyes and innocent faces, invaded the pantry, often leaping from silverware drawers when she opened them. Flying termites drifted in piles on the steps where African children popped them raw into their mouths, eating them like peanuts. Then those strange marching insects with big pinchers came out after the first rains—the kind children were fond of placing together in glass jars to watch a good fight.

And spiders. On their first night in the new house, Kay was sitting at the dining table with a spoonful of custard poised in front of her mouth when at eye-level on the wall across the room she saw a huge flat spider. Leigh, their ten-year-old daughter must have seen it at the same time; they both screamed.

Charles recovered from his surprise and scolded, "Don't be silly. Those spiders are harmless and quite useful. They eat malaria mosquitoes."

"Will the spiders get malaria, daddy?" Leigh asked.

Kay wasn't impressed, but later she rather enjoyed the antics of those lovely spiders hanging on the ceiling like dark stars.

The most shocking discovery was a hive of wild African bees that had taken residence in the chimney. On cool nights, they were quiet, but during midday heat, they filtered down through the fireplace and buzzed to exhaustion in the living room. Bush babies, squeezing slender bodies through holes in screens, braved the presence of humans for a free meal. When Kay swept the bees still buzzing and convulsing into the dustpan, Leigh begged her to leave them.

"I like to watch bush babies eat bees," she giggled. "They hop about so funny when they get stung."

Later, when Leigh got stung, the bees weren't funny. The poison from a single sting made a swelling the size of a fist. That same day, Abelo coaxed Kay outside into the garden to look at bees, and, pointing to the chimney, said, "Madam, the bees find that a good place."

Knowing how dangerous wild African bees can be, Kay said," Yes, indeed. We'll have to do something about that."

The battle began.

Abelo tried various ways to get rid of bees. He popped their heads with his fingernails and swept them into dustpans. He built a roaring fire in the fireplace, but bees abandoned the hive only while the heat was on. He tried to smoke them out by burning damp grass in the fireplace. The bees left momentarily, hovered around the chimney, and returned when the smoke died down. Leigh, who is easy-going like her father, ignored the persistent buzzing around her head and feet and at the window screens while doing her homework in the living room.

Meanwhile, Charles was away most of the time living somewhere in the bush or in a remote area of a game park gathering statistics on hyenas. One weekend he came home long enough to replenish his supplies of canned food, chocolate bars, and clean underwear.

"You must help us do something about the bee situation," Kay said at dinner. "We have a hive of wild African bees in our chimney in the living room and our lives are in danger."

"Aw, honey," Charles said, laughing at his own pun. "It can't be that bad. We're just lucky we don't have bats in our belfry."

"It's nearly Christmas," Leigh reminded him. "Think of all the places Santa might get stung coming down the chimney."

They both laughed, but Kay didn't think it was funny.

After Charles drove away in the Land Rover on Monday morning, Kay called the African Studies Institute which, in turn, called the Lusaka Fire Department. Late that afternoon, a fire truck came roaring up the driveway to assess the situation. The firemen looked impressive in navy blue uniforms and official red hats. Leigh had just come home from school and was delighted with all the excitement.

Six firemen came again after dark to exterminate the bees

while they were "sleeping." Two firemen climbed upon the roof to spray carbon tetrachloride down the chimney, and two went inside to spray up the chimney while two firemen watched and made jokes about bees. Then they zoomed away in the dark after assuring Kay she would have "no more troubles." But her troubles were just beginning.

A few days later, Abelo called Kay into the garden again and pointed to the chimney. "Madam," he said, "the bees are not finished."

Kay felt discouraged. "What would you suggest we do?"

"Move out of this house," Abelo said. "Bees can be very dangerous."

Kay looked at him; he was serious. "We can't," she said. "We have no place to go."

A strange new development distracted Kay from concentrating on bees. Live maggots, feasting off the rotting bee hive in the chimney, began to drop from the ceiling. They fell from a plugged opening beside the chimney used in colonial days to connect a wood-burning stove. For three days, maggots rained down making small clicking sounds on impact. There was nothing to do but assign maggot sweepers; Leigh and Kay took turns when Abelo was busy. If the maggots were left to their own devices, some built-in guide directed them to migrate across the kitchen, through the dining room, down the hall, and out the crack under the front door. Since nobody was willing to lose sleep to keep maggot watch, live maggots crunched underfoot when Kay came downstairs each morning.

As mysteriously as the maggots came, they disappeared. Then dirty honey oozed in rivulets down the wall from the plugged opening. Some dripped on the stove and some made its way through rafters and dripped from the ceiling. Kay placed buckets under the drips while Abelo wiped walls, but they played a losing game. Ants, flies, and roaches came to sip at the poisoned honey even as Abelo cleaned it up. After collecting a quart of the sweet, sooty gook, Kay filed another complaint with the Institute, but plugged toilets took precedence over dripping honey.

Charles came home over the weekend and laughed when he saw the condition of the kitchen.

"Wait till I tell you about the maggots!" Kay said.

He laughed again. "I was looking forward to some good home-cooked food, but fried maggots in honey wasn't exactly what I had in mind."

Kay was furious that he never took anything seriously. If she hadn't been so glad to see him, she would have insisted he cook his own maggots.

On Monday, Kay called the Lusaka Fire Department again. The firemen refused to believe the bees had returned. "Come and see for yourselves," Kay insisted. "We're in great danger here. We could be mortally stung. There are so many."

Shortly after dark, the fire truck roared up the driveway again with six big firemen. They rushed in carrying galvanized tubs and more spray. They unplugged the stove flue and removed rotting honeycomb and bees. Working with long poles, they poked honey and honeycomb down the chimney and into the fireplace where a tall, broad-shouldered fireman shoveled it into a tub. He seemed to enjoy himself as he examined the contents of each shovel. Presently, he shouted, "Look at the king bee!" He pointed to the large queen still intact and encased in a sticky jell.

"That's the queen bee," Kay said.

"Oh, no!" he insisted. "That is the king bee and he has all these wives."

Kay knew it was useless to try to convince him. While he

carried out two tubs of rotting debris, she wondered how many wives he had tucked away in mud huts in the village.

A week later, Abelo was in the garden pointing to the chimney. "Madam," he called. "The bees still find that a good place."

Kay nodded. She had seen them. Drawn by the odor of honey, a new hive had taken residence. She was too embarrassed to call the fire department again; She hoped if she ignored the bees, they might go away.

For several months Kay resigned herself to living as harmoniously with bees as possible, hoping no calamity would occur before the end of the year. Christmas came and went and so did Easter. Her state of mind was not eased when she read in the Lusaka News that a village man had died when attacked by wild bees.

One evening just before dark, the bees descended upon them with a vengeance. Leigh, doing homework at a table in the living room, called with panic in her voice. "Hey, Mom! Come and look! There are so many bees!"

Kay hurried in to find roaring, excited bees pouring out of the fireplace. She grabbed Leigh by the arm and dragged her from the room. "My books!" Leigh protested. "I don't want them to get stung. The bees might make them into honeycomb."

"Forget the homework!" Kay screamed, "You'll be killed. Get out!"

She slammed the door behind them but bees bombed under the cracks beneath the doors. She packed bath towels in the cracks and ran to the telephone. The housing office was closed. She was afraid to call the Lusaka Fire Department again. They would consider her neurotic and wouldn't believe her; they thought they had solved her problem.

She lay awake during the night listening to a roar like the droning of a jet engine. Sometime past midnight, she eased her head through the door and marveled at nature. Angry, hysterical bees buzzed on chairs, tables, and the mantle piece, covering the floor, furniture and light fixtures in a solid mass.

After breakfast, Kay waded cautiously into the living room to retrieve Leigh's homework, shaking her books and papers free of inert bees with a thumb and forefinger. Leigh, following behind her, called out in a tone that would have made her father proud. "Look, Mom! Wall-to-wall bees!"

She was right. The bees had buzzed themselves lifeless; most were lying dead or exhausted on the tables and floor. A few, still active, straggled drunkenly out of the chimney, and Kay knew their troubles were just beginning.

After getting Leigh off to school, she called the Institute's housing office. Mr. Patel, the director, informed her she would have to come in to file a complaint and the matter would be taken care of as soon as possible. From past experience, she knew "as soon as possible" might be a matter of days, weeks, months.

"Please try to understand," Kay pleaded. "Wild bees have swarmed in my living room. We're in great danger here."

"You must be mistaken," Mr. Patel said with a thick British and East Indian accent. "Wild bees swarm outside."

"Please," she begged, "Send somebody at once to make a report. This is an emergency. My living room is wall-to-wall with bees."

"You might call the Fire Department," Mr. Patel said. "We don't have the equipment or personnel to handle emergencies."

Kay called the Lusaka Fire Department again and talked to Mr. Zulu, the fire chief, who recognized her name. He laughed when she told him about the swarm.

"Bees swarm outside," he said.

"These bees are inside," Kay said. "I have wall-to-wall bees in my living room."

He laughed again. "The bees want to start a new village."

"Yes, I know. But can't you do something?"

"Maybe tomorrow they will go away."

"We can't wait," Kay insisted. "My daughter's life is in danger."

She listened to the accelerated rumbling of bees behind her with one ear and the other pressed to the receiver while Mr. Zulu lectured on the habits and habitats of bees before he agreed to send a truck out after dark.

When the fire truck arrived at dusk, the main swarm had clustered on a bougainvillaea bush outside the patio door, hanging lush and ripe like poison pear-shaped fruit. The firemen sprayed the swarm and told her they were paid to put out fires, not kill bees, and the Institute would have to "do something."

Kay relayed the message to Mr. Patel.

"What would you suggest we do?" he asked. She couldn't decide from his tone whether he was being sarcastic or really wanted suggestions.

"Now that bees are out of the chimney," she said, "this would be a good time to tie a screen across the top. The odor of honey will attract other swarms if we don't do that."

There was a long pause on the other end of the line. "I can send someone out," he said. "Tomorrow morning."

Next morning an old Mercedes truck rattled up the driveway. A crew of twelve men climbed off a flatbed in back, and the truck sped away. Kay stood at the kitchen window, watching. Workers had arrived empty-handed—no screening, no ladder, no tools. The men drifted toward the back of the house, looked up at the steep roof, and shook their heads. Then they squatted by the washtubs, chattering in Nyanja. For most of an hour, they looked up at the chimney, shook their heads, clicked their tongues, and emitted low rumbling sounds. Soon the truck returned, sat vibrating in the driveway while the twelve men climbed aboard, revved its engine and roared away. Nothing had been done.

If Charles had been home, he probably would have laughed, but Kay was furious. She had been patient; she had waited almost a year for a solution to her problem.

"If an entire crew of men can't do one small job," Kay fumed at Abelo, " then I'll do it myself. I'm going to climb up on that roof and get it done."

"Oh, no, Madam," he begged. He place his hands together, an anxious frown on his face. "That is too dangerous."

By Friday afternoon, Kay had collected a ladder, a piece of strong wire, a length of screening, and a pair of pliers. She was ready to go to work. Looking up, she realized the house was taller and the roof steeper than she had thought. Her stomach felt queazy, but she was determined. She tied the pliers around her waist with the strip of wire and knotted a length of heavy twine to the light screening, tying the other end to her wrist. She removed her sneakers and placed them beside the concrete tubs, remembering from her childhood years as a tomboy that bare feet have better grip. But she had misjudged the height of the roof; the ladder didn't reach the eaves. She dragged the ladder sideways until it touched the copper drain pipe. She shook the pipe vigorously, testing for strength. It seemed steady enough to hold her, but when she reached the top of the ladder and threw her weight upon it, her heart almost stopped. She heard the pipe crack but swung lightly upon it and reached for a precarious grip on the edge of the roof. The shingles were old; she hoped they wouldn't break.

She hadn't realized how out of shape she was. Her arms ached as she drew her body upward. She tried to forget the weight of the pliers around her waist and the tug of the twine at her wrist. She heard the seams of her jeans rip when she threw her left leg over the shingled eaves, rolled on to the roof, and got a firm grip with her toes. At last she was balanced. She moved sideways, crablike, toward the gutter at the gable and inched her way up the steep incline, testing each move with fingers and toes. When she reached the top, she swung her leg over the ridge, straddled the peak, and fished the screen up with the twine tied to her wrist. Drawing herself, inch by inch, toward the chimney, she leaned upon it.

It took only minutes to shape screening over the top. Drawing wire around the edges of the second row of brick, she pulled tight to prevent any loose edges where bees might find their way inside. Even as she worked, two yellow bees bombed against the screen and took off. She tied the wire and twisted it with pliers, satisfied the plan was going to work. The screen sagged a little but the job was done, and she had been able to do something a crew of twelve men had not. Smiling, she let the pliers slide down the steep roof, listening to the washboard effect as they rumbled down the shingles and struck with a metallic clink on the concrete below. Then she looked around her at the magnificent view from the roof.

Along the front driveway, bougainvillaea which had not been trimmed for years cascaded over the fence in unruly masses of color—fushia, lavender, burgundy, rusty orange. Hardy climbing roses decorated a peeling white trellis with splashes of green and bright red, and a poinsettia tree in full bloom stood in the corner beside them. To the left, beyond a cluster of jacaranda trees, the small houses of the workers for the Institute stood in neat rows, and to the right, an orchard of fruit trees — orange, lemon, guava, mango. In the back garden, a pair of frangipani trees framed a thatched shelter, their fleshy, succulent branches reaching out like stubby fingers. And farther beyond, was Kaunda Square where thousands of workers had migrated from villages and built modest homes. Viewing the world from above, she breathed in the odor of roses and felt detached and serene, the kind of high a mountain climber might feel when reaching a distant peak.

Kay turned at the sound of a roaring engine. A big hook-and-ladder truck from the Lusaka Fire Department came zooming down the dirt road in a cloud of orange dust. It swung in a wide curve and turned into the driveway of the Institute. Puzzled, she looked about, searching for flames or smoke and saw Abelo outside the front door, arms flailing, pointing to the fire truck.

"Don't jump, Madam," he called. "We will save you. I called for help."

Kay's moment of triumph turned to humiliation. The big firemen in blue uniforms had come to her rescue for what she hoped would be the last time. While workers from the Institute drifted out of buildings to watch, men cranked the tall ladder to the peaked ridge of the house.

Straddling the ridge of the roof, Kay worked her way to the edge and looked down. A fireman was on his way up. She wanted to tell him she was perfectly capable of coming down alone, but decided against it. She let him sling her over his shoulder and carry her down where other firemen stood shaking their heads and clucking their tongues. Mr. Zulu shook her hand and congratulated the men on getting her down safely. Abelo stood to one side, proud and smiling, convinced he had saved her from disaster. She was grateful neither Charles nor Leigh were home at the time; she knew they would have laughed.

THE SHAPING OF KASINDA

Kasinda got the idea for the gift one Saturday morning when he went with his mother to ZOK, the biggest government store in Lusaka which stood for "Zambia is OK." Sometimes, he wanted to stay in the compound at Kaunda Square to play with his friends, but his mother always insisted he go with her to care for his little sister, Egenesi. Although they didn't talk about it, he knew his mother needed him to be with her if she had a seizure. His health teacher at school had told him seizures were caused by damage to the brain, but his father had run away believing his mother was possessed with evil spirits.

At first, Kasinda thought she went to ZOK because she liked the crowds and the excitement, but one day he noticed she stopped, as she always did, at the counter where the shining metal pots were displayed in rows upon the shelves. He watched her face as she lifted the gleaming lid by the black knob, examined the inside, ran her fingers over the smooth surface, and held the pot at arm's length, laughing at her reflection on the polished steel.

"How pretty my mother is when she is happy!" he thought. In his imagination, he could see her cooking maize in that pot, and he decided to find a way to buy it.

"Do you like the pot, Mother?" he asked softly as he tightened his fingers on Egenesi's hand to keep her from running about the store.

"*Etu,*" she responded, making a guttural sound of pleasure low in her throat. "But it is very dear."

"How many *kwachas*?" he asked.

"Many, many *kwachas*," she said, squinting at the numbers on the tag as she spoke. "I think it is twelve."

Kasinda caught his breath, his eyes big with surprise. He thought of the fine clay pots his grandmother made in the village from wet clay she carried from the river and which she gave to his mother for nothing.

"That is almost as much as I earn in a month selling soap and wild greens at the market in Kaunda Square," his mother said, placing the pot back on the shelf. "But it is pretty to see."

Riding home on the bus that day, Kasinda played games with imagination. He had not seen other women in his neighborhood at Kaunda Square with a pot like that one, and he knew they would be envious. He saw himself presenting the gleaming pot with the black knob on top to his mother as a gift, and he smiled at the image of her expressions of joy and surprise. He felt a great swelling of pride when, in his mind, he saw neighbors admiring it and his mother saying, "My son, Kasinda bought it for me. He is very clever."

Kasinda decided on that day he would find work to buy the pot for his mother. Now, after many weeks, he carried the box carefully under his arm as he walked along the road. The gift meant appreciation for his mother who had carried him in her womb and had nursed him from her body during the famine. It was she who sat beside him on his sleeping mat those long nights when he almost died from fever. It was she who worked to feed him and pay his school fees after his father went away. The gift also represented his mother's joy in him, her only living son, and her pride in knowing he would some day be strong enough to protect her and provide for her.

Most of all, the gift represented many hours of hard work. At first, the task seemed a simple one, but when he began to look for odd jobs, he found reaching his goal almost impossible. Many grown men were looking for employment. Even his father, an honest village man, had not been able to find steady work. Nobody wanted to hire a boy. At one time, he thought of trying to steal the pot, but he knew his mother would not want him to be a thief to get it.

Kasinda did not tell anyone except his mother when he went into the city alone to look for work. She looked worried and warned him about getting into trouble. Sometimes she reminded him she needed a son's help at her stall in the market, but Kasinda was determined to reach his goal. He helped a man polish and repair shoes at the big city market, he ran errands for women who owned small stores or kiosks, and he washed cars for a man who provided him with a pail and a soft cloth. On days when there was no work, he swallowed his shame and begged for coins on the street.

Usually, he went without food and walked home in the evening to save bus fare. At night, when his mother wasn't watching, he hid the coins he had earned in a special place. The collection grew until one day there was enough to buy the shining pot. The work had been harder than he expected. If he could not feel the package pressing against his side, he would not believe he had actually bought the pot with money he had earned. Soon it would belong to his mother.

Kasinda's legs were tired. He had walked all the way from main street in Lusaka to his township with the precious package under his arm. After he bought bright wrapping paper and a red ribbon, he didn't have enough money to ride the bus home. He imagined the look of great joy on his mother's face when she saw the gift. He was the man of the house, and he wanted to help support her, give her nice things.

Before Kasinda reached the compound, he began to feel

uneasy. He knew someone was sick; the frantic rhythm of the distant drums told him this was so. He felt the first throbbing from far away in the early twilight, but the faint vibrations blended with the blasts of trucks along the road. Gradually, the pattern of the rhythm drew pictures in his mind of people dancing, shaking rattles, and beating on pots and pieces of wood to frighten away evil spirits.

Fear stirred pains in the pit of his stomach at the thought his mother might have had a seizure, and he was not there to care for her. He quickened his pace, hoping his fear would not be realized, but when he came in sight of his house, he saw a light inside and women dancing beside the door. He entered and found his mother lying on a mat. Her eyes were closed. She seemed to be sleeping. He was tired from his long walk, and weak from hunger. The penetrating throb of the big drums inside the little house made his head ache; sharp pains shot through his ears.

"Is my mother all right?" he asked Violeti, a women who lived next door. He was forced to yell to make himself heard above the pulsating noise. He read the woman's lips with great effort in the dim light as she answered, "She was sick, but now she is resting."

Kasinda hesitated, torn between wanting to run away and wanting to wake his mother at once to show her the gift in front of all the people. With great strength, he forced himself to be patient. This was a day he had worked and waited for; surely he was strong enough to wait a little longer. He went outside and sat with his back against the house, still clutching the package in his arms. He closed his eyes, submitting to the even beat of the drums, the flow of voices, the measured movements of dancers.

He awoke when his mother placed her hand on his arm, shaking him gently. It was morning!

"You looked so tired," she said, "I did not want to wake you, but you must not sleep here unprotected."

Consciousness spread over him like the slow dawning of the day. At first he was confused, then he remembered. He searched his mother's face to make certain she had recovered, then he looked for the package. It was gone!

"Mother! Mother!" he cried in panic. "Did you take it?"

"Take what?" his mother asked.

"The gift!"

"There is no gift," she said, her voice almost a whisper.

"Yes," he cried. "I bought a gift yesterday in the city. It was for you!"

His mother smiled at his confusion. "You must be dreaming," she said. "Come, you will feel better after you have eaten."

The sun was high in the sky, but Kasinda still sat with his back pressed against the cinder-block wall of the little house, his skinny legs drawn up in a bow, his head on his arms, his eyes closed tight. Fear, anger, helplessness flowed through every fiber of his body. There seemed to be evil spirits working against him. He had tried. Yes, he had really tried to do a good thing. He thought of his father and wondered if this was the way his father felt when he walked away and left them without a word. It wasn't easy to become a man.

Elephant Kill

"They've killed an elephant," Mateyo called, hurrying to Joel Wade's hut on the edge of Chikumbe Village in Eastern Zambia. A boyish smile transformed his oval face; his perfect teeth glistened. His usually subdued voice was vibrant with excitement of the kill.

Joel was washing breakfast dishes in a green plastic bucket on the tailgate of his battered Land Rover. His oily blond hair hung below the red baseball cap he wore to shade his eyes from tropical glare. "Where?" he asked, squinting into sun. He turned his tin cup and bowl upside down on a towel and shook his hands dry.

"There," Mateyo said, pointing with a skinny index finger.

Joel threw his dish water on a cactus bush beside his hut and hung the cloth on a nail inside the door. His interpreter's characteristic vagueness annoyed him. "Who killed an elephant?"

"The game guard."

"I thought killing an elephant was illegal except on government-approved safaris."

Joel felt under the cot for his briefcase with a big freckled hand.

"Elephants outside the tsetse fly control fence have to be killed."

"Is that so?" Joel said, sorting through papers in his briefcase.

"Yes. They infect other animals."

"What does the game guard do with the tusks?" He knew the ivory would be worth a fortune to the game guard on the black market.

"The government owns the ivory," Mateyo said. "The guard must sell the tusks to the government."

"What happens to the meat?"

"People eat the meat."

Joel stroked the short beard he had let grow since coming to Chikumbe and indulged in a moment of envy. Since arriving in Zambia, he had ached to go on a hunting safari. His father had taken him rabbit hunting when he was a boy, and he still remembered the feel of the polished wood as he ran his hands over the stock of his father's big gun. He recalled the thrill of sighting through the barrel of the new .22 he got for his twelfth birthday and of seeing rabbits topple and roll over when he made a hit. He remembered with affection the look of pride on his father's face as they trudged together through crisp autumn fields of stubble with rabbits slung over their shoulders.

Twenty years later and half a world away, he had driven through Nsefu game reservation on his way to Chikumbe and was thrilled at the sight of antelope and zebras grazing together in a draw near a water hole . . . and of springbok prinking across the veld just asking to be brought down like those rabbits racing across wheat stubble back home in Kansas. . . and elephant herds traveling between clusters of forests looking from a distance like great wooly mammoths right out of the ice age. Lord, how he wanted to be the man who killed that elephant! His dream of big game hunting had influenced him to do agricultural research in Central Africa rather than Southeast Asia. He pushed his baseball cap back from his forehead, and sighed. Well, he had a job to do and work came first.

"Please, sir. Can we go?" Mateyo paced between the patch of tall cactus and the tailgate of the Land Rover, his forehead creased, his eyes drooping, and his mouth still pursed on the word "go." "I need meat for my family."

Joel remembered that Mateyo, hardly more than a child himself, had a wife and child in a nearby village. He suppressed a chuckle when he saw the comical expression on Mateyo's face.

"Nobody will be in the village today," Mateyo added. "They'll all be at the elephant kill."

"I suppose so," Joel said. "How far?"

"Cimbuna said three kilometers."

A smile flooded Mateyo's face as Joel put his dishes in a plastic bag, transferred food boxes from the Land Rover to his sleeping hut, hung his camera over his shoulder and slipped a note pad into the pocket of his baggy bush-jeans.

At the sound of the motor, Yesiteli rushed out of her hut with her baby on her back and a large white basin on her head. She climbed into the back of the Land Rover beaming at the thought of getting a ride and bared her breast to nurse her baby. The basin which she placed beside her was filled with corn meal tied in a cloth. Yesiteli lived in a hut beside Joel's with her husband, Yelisani. She was Yelisani's only wife and had given birth to thirteen children. Because of Yesiteli's resourceful nurturing and Yelisani's dependability as a husband, all thirteen children survived. Joel knew he was being dangerously subjective for a researcher, but he didn't care. Plump and jolly Yesiteli was his favorite village mother and nearest to his ideal of what a good mother ought to be.

Cimbuna and Kabuula, two village men, got into the back seat and offered to serve as guides. "Cimbuna wants you to stop at the tsetse fly control gate to ask directions," Mateyo said after much animated conversation in Nyanja.

"The guards know everything," Mateyo explained as Joel stopped in front of the log blockade. "People passing this way tell them all the news and they like to give advice."

The two uniformed guards argued rapidly in Nyanja. "Three kilometers," the tallest guard said suddenly in English, extending his long arm toward an open field. He gave a military salute and motioned Joel to drive on.

Someone had misunderstood. The beginning of the road leading to the elephant kill was three kilometers, not the elephant itself. Joel turned into a lane where grass grew between two worn tire tracks. Elephant grass, acacia, and small baobab crowded in on either side. Bushes scraped the wheels, the windshield, and the sides of the Land Rover as he plowed through. Seven kilometers later, he paused where two grassy lanes crossed.

Mateyo, Cimbuna, and Kabuula argued politely about which way to go. While Joel waited for their decision, he saw an African in a bright blue shirt running up the path waving a *phwitika* to attract attention. Joel felt uneasy at the sight of the long sharp blade until he recognized the man as Mcabe, an occasional visitor to Chikumbe. He waited for Mcabe to get on board. After more animated conversations, Mateyo announced, "Mcabe says he knows exactly where the elephant is and will be our guide."

Paths deteriorated into bush, slowing progress. An Ngoni tribesman came toward them through the forest. He wore English shorts, was bare from the waist up, and his stolid face was framed by unclipped hair standing out six to eight inches in all directions. Wooden pegs filled large holes in his earlobes. He carried a spear in one hand and a *phwitika* in the other. He also climbed aboard, and when bushes became too thick for travel, he and Mcabe climbed out to slice them down with their long blades.

"We're lucky to have them with us," Mateyo said, but Joel wasn't sure. He silently cursed himself for his gullibility, for allowing himself to be drawn into a wild and futile chase. Joel knew he was driving blindly into deep forests where he had no survival skills and was completely dependent upon the two armed men in back; the thought chilled him.

Suddenly, a boulder bigger than the Land Rover loomed before him. Elephant spoor spotted the grass; a large tree lay on its side freshly uprooted. "From here we walk," Joel announced. He clicked on the hand brake, cut the ignition, and slipped the keys into the pocket of his bush jeans, buttoning the flap.

Standing on the hood of the Land Rover, Joel looked out over the basin of the Lutumbwe River. A line of green trees and low vegetation followed the irregular thread of the river, a pleasing contrast to cactus plants, brown grass, and tortured trees growing around Chikumbe village.

The Ngoni led the party to the left following the rim of the river basin. Mcabe followed behind, pausing to hack a trail by marking both sides of trees at a distance of ten paces. Joel watched Mcabe and counted the markings. He struggled to keep up with his barefoot companions. Yesiteli, who carried her baby and a basin of corn meal, gradually fell behind. Joel turned at Yesiteli's shrill greeting to a group of women walking single-file on a path from the river with water jars on their heads.

Shots rang out; loud crashing echoed through the forest. The women screamed, scattered, and fled through the trees like a flock of bright-colored birds.

"Elephants!" Mateyo called to Joel. "Come with me!"

Joel turned, waiting for Yesiteli.

"Hurry!" Mateyo insisted.

Joel saw Yesiteli jogging around the side of a giant termite hill. She steadied the basin on her head with both hands. Her fat cheeks, her full breasts, and the silent wide-eyed baby on her back flopped about comically. He ran with her in the direction of the kill.

A crowd of African men, perhaps a hundred, were gathered in quiet groups about the elephant, a mammoth gray bull lying on its side. Its trunk was severed to show it had been killed and had not died of disease. Joel saw the great bulk of its wrinkled body, still and lifeless upon decaying leaves, and was moved by its massive beauty. Its torso mounded against the tortured landscape of splintered trees. The legs, recumbent and erected horizontally in pairs, extended like tree trunks, but the trunk itself lay scarlet tipped and limp beside curved tusks of pale ivory. Joel wanted this magnificent animal to be alive and felt ambivalence toward the man who killed it—the man he suspected might have killed for ivory.

Joel turned his attention to the celebration around him. Men squatted in groups talking in low voices. Some walked around the huge animal evaluating it critically, lips pursed, heads inclined. Others stood with one foot propped on the tusks or upon the bulky legs. A group of men on the fringe of the gathering cut saplings and built a drying rack for meat, constructing it as a lean-to with poles for support and tied smaller poles across the main frame with narrow strips of bark from the *msendaluzi* tree. Another group, working in silence, built a fire beneath the rack. When the work was finished, they squatted again in groups, talked, waited.

Joel squatted with the men. He had learned the gift of patience in the village. Without clocks, the sense of time was different and events took place when he least expected them. He noticed the women had gathered in large groups about fifty feet away. Some sat in closed circles, visiting as they often did in villages. Some gathered firewood, built cooking fires, or nursed babies. Others carried water from the river in cooking pots balanced on their heads. Yesiteli had melted into the colorful crowd. Her husband, Yelisani, had come early that morning and was standing near the elephant holding his *phwitika* ready to work, ready to provide for his family.

"Why are so many women and children here?" Joel asked.

"Women come to cook fresh meat for husbands who will be assigned by the game guard to carve the elephant," Mateyo said. "Most meat will be dried a short time on the drying rack to keep away insects. Later it will be dried for a long time over charcoal fires in villages." He paused and pointed to a small group of women hovering near the kill. "They are widows," Mateyo said. "It is our custom to give widows the liver and other soft parts which cannot be dried."

"Why is everybody staring at me?" Joel asked.

"You're different," Mateyo said. "Some people here have never seen a white man."

Men lined up to shake his hand, and then women came, pumping his hand, clucking pleasantries, smiling. Before the ceremony was finished, a young barefoot African in an English tweed overcoat and a battered fedora with the crown missing stepped upon a large volcanic stone to make a speech. Joel was puzzled at the man's scolding, reproachful tone. He waved his arms and his voice rose and fell in dramatic oratory. Women slunk away, humiliated, chastised.

"What's going on, Mateyo? What's he saying?"

"He is saying our president brought you from the United States to learn about the people of Africa. He is saying we must make a good impression on you and not be a nuisance."

Joel was annoyed. "Why is he saying that? Your president doesn't know I exist!"

"If they think our president sent you, you will be safe," Mateyo said. "I told him to say that. Some people may not like you because you are different." Mateyo walked away; the conversation was finished.

The sun was directly overhead when all eyes turned toward the river; the game guard arrived. He looked impressive in his khaki uniform, a World War I army uniform complete with wrapped leggings, broad brimmed hat, and an obsolete rifle slung over his shoulder. He strode through the crowd with an air of propriety, laughing and talking, while barefoot men looked on and listened with respect.

"He is saying," Mateyo told Joel, "that a male, female, and a half-grown elephant crossed to this side of the river into the tsetse fly area. This is the male which he had no trouble killing, but the mother and the son escaped. When he found them, he shot the mother three times. That was the noise we heard in the forest on our way here. He says the mother fell on her side, but her young son helped her to her feet and propped her up. Before he could shoot the mother again, her young son chased him to the river where he has been hiding near the water."

Perhaps the words "young son" troubled Joel, or perhaps it was the calf's touching attempt to save its mother; he couldn't be sure. He had always been interested in people; it had never seemed important to him that animals might have intelligence, feelings, family loyalties. He watched the game guard strut among admiring villagers, telling his story, savoring his words. Joel watched him reenact the drama of the hunt, puzzled by the ambivalence burning inside him.

Looking important and composed, the game guard took a small notebook from his shirt pocket to record the names of workers. He organized three teams, men from different villages, who began work upon the great carcass. Yelisani, waist-bare and wet-washed with sweat, leaped upon the broad belly and paused for balance, a glistening statue of living obsidian. With rippling muscles, he raised his ancient axe and hacked a cross upon the mammoth's rump, peeled back the lice infested skin, exposing white membrane underneath. He placed the leathery side in squares against the ground and stacked the tenderloin and strips of red meat.

The other workers joined him two by two, hacking other crosses in their turn. The second team carved the shoulder meat and stripped the collar bone while a worker chopped the trunk into pot-sized pieces and sent children running with them to the fires. The third team worked from the elephant's spine, exposing the vertebrae and picking flesh away. They cut the meat in layers along the upper ribs and arranged the strips neatly upon the squares of skin. The Ngoni tribesman Joel had seen along the trail worked on the back section, his chest and face spattered with blood; he appeared more fierce and savage than when Joel saw him strolling through the woods. Shivers of horror quivered along Joel's spine as he watched the Ngoni hack at the hind quarters and strip the rump to the testicles—testicles as large and brown as inflated basketballs.

Phwitika action cut a thin, clean line sliding easily from testicles to throat, releasing stomach gas with explosive flatulence. Internal pressure forced the entrails out; and while the juices oozed, the topside crew disengaged the ribs. Yelisani helped arrange the viscera in a loose mass upon the ground; he stood blood-smeared and smiling among the stench and slime, satisfied. Soon he hacked intestines into strips, emptied them of half-digested leaves and cut them into nature's biggest chitterlings.

Widows came to claim the liver meat. Begging and clucking, they rushed two men straining to lift the huge organ impaled upon a pole, hanging like a flower, bunched and blossoming on its giant stem. Women, watching from a modest distance, sent children scurrying for pieces of tender meat and added twigs to small fires built between jagged rocks. The children hurried back, clutching bloody chunks that dripped against distended bellies.

"They have not tasted meat for many months," Mateyo murmured. "They are happy now."

Yelisani, tired from work and weak from hunger, threaded chunks of leg meat on his *phwitika* and sent his daughter to cook them at the fire. Joel watched him pace and then devour raw flesh with sweat and blood dripping down his arm. Three men carried rotting logs to feed the fire beneath the drying rack. They gathered strips of meat, lay them across the inclined frame, and squatted near the fire. Joel sat upon a tree trunk, taking notes. He watched the smoke curl upward, linger about the edge of the drying frame, and seep through cracks between layers of red, raw meat. He turned his eyes to the carcass, half consumed, lying like a great wound in the earth; the stripped rib cage lay bare against the fading light.

The carvers paused and began to drift away. "When will the workers turn the elephant over and carve the other side?" Joel asked.

"Tomorrow," Mateyo said. "Men will stand guard tonight."

"How much of the elephant will the people eat?"

"Everything."

"I mean, what will be left when the carving is finished?"

"Only a few bones."

Mateyo bought meat from the game guard and turned toward the setting sun. "We must go," he said, "while there is still light to follow the trail. You would not be safe here tonight."

"There's no hurry," Joel said, unafraid, but he knew night can descend suddenly near the equator. He returned the notebook to the pocket of his bush jeans and followed his guides, looking back only once at the village people busy with preparations to sleep among the rubble of stones.

Later that night, after a meal of canned stew, Joel sat in a folding chair beside his outdoor cooking fire. A feeling of well-being settled over him as he listened to comforting sounds coming from huts and kitchens—sounds of people settling in for the night. Children sat on a log near his fire chanting to music from his battery radio. Above their soft harmony, one voice stood out. It was the voice of a child crying.

"What's wrong?" Joel asked the children.

"Tezewanthu is crying." A boy said in broken English. "She misses her mother."

"Who is her mother?"

"Yesiteli. She couldn't take Tezewanthu with her to the kill. The baby is too heavy."

Tezewanthu's ragged dress was caked with dust, but Joel wrapped her in a bath towel and sat beside the fire holding her in his arms, resting her head against his shoulder. As she drifted into sleep, Joel felt the measured rhythm of her shallow breathing and stared into the fire which had burned to glowing embers.

Joel's thoughts turned to things men are slow to talk about unless they are under the open sky where stars seem to burn a pathway to the center of the universe. He thought about the need to kill and be killed, the need to eat and be eaten. The warm child in his arms reminded him of the needs of children, and the need of the elephant calf to protect his mother. His desire to kill an elephant dissolved in the darkness behind him. He felt humbled by the indomitable spirit of intelligent animals against unfair and uneven odds, their will to survive, the resilience of life. Yet, soon, he thought, there may be no more living elephants. They will be only a memory.

Joel imagined men standing guard around the elephant beside the muddy river to protect it from hyenas, a carcass half consumed and scarlet against the flames of small fires burning like red eyes of the forest. He saw the ragged half-naked men squatting to feed the fire beneath the inclined sapling frame sagging beneath the weight of coarse-grained meat; pale smoke curled upward, lingered at the edge, drifted through crevasses and disappeared into night. It could have been a scene from any age at some place on the earth since the dawn of early man.

Joel imagined that tomorrow, before sundown, Yesiteli would come striding into the village carrying her baby on her back and a heavy basin of meat upon her head, walking behind her husband as was her custom. And Joel would say to her in greeting, as he always did when she came home from working in the fields, "Are you tired?" And after walking miles through the forest with a heavy load, Yesiteli would answer, as she always did, "Only my legs.

Silver Bowls

Sendeu ole Mbarnoti's grandson, Mbatyani, had graduated from the local mission school against his wishes and had learned to speak English. Now Sendeu was glad that this was so; there was someone to "eat the news" with him and warn him about threats to the Maasai people. Mbatyani told him the government built a road through their valley so white men could drive vehicles to the silver bowls on the flat plains below Susua Crater, a story impossible to believe. He said white ladders reached as high as the buzzard flies and great silver bowls on top listened for things in the sky.

"Are they listening for God?" Sendeu asked.

"No," his grandson said. "They are listening for things in outer space."

Sendeu's eyes grew wide then narrowed as he studied the hills. The only space he knew was the distant haze along the mountain ridge where mist gathered morning and evening and the wide open sky blazed with heat at midday. If they weren't listening for God, it seemed a foolish thing to do with so much to be done on earth. There were children to feed and cattle to herd.

"Take me to see this thing," Sendeu said.

"But grandfather, it's too far. You're not strong enough to walk a full day's journey." Mbatyani noticed Sendeu now leaned more on his stick for walking, and often sat for hours on the large red stone on the side of the crater where he watched the village and herders from a distance.

"You're insulting me," Sendeu grumbled. "I'm as strong as I ever was." Mbatyani knew it was useless to argue with his grandfather. In Sendeu's mind he would always be a warrior.

They started walking in early morning, following the road west across the Rift Valley. They passed through grassy plains where ostriches fed, their thin legs supporting heavy bodies as they chased each other at great speed. Farther along, in thickets of twisted yellow thorn, a family of giraffes nibbled at prickly branches of thorn trees, and when they entered grasslands again, a herd of zebra grazed at a distance. As the sun climbed higher and day grew yellow with heat, game found places to rest in shade. Mbatyani and his grandfather were alone on the road except for an occasional vehicle carrying transport between Naivasha and Narok.

For many miles, Sendeu walked with his back straight and his head held high like a true Maasai. Mbatyani loved his grandfather and wanted to please him but knew he had been a disappointment. He, Mbatyani, was the only grandson rebellious enough to leave the reserve to go to school. Years ago, when Mbatyani was a *laioni*, a small boy too young to be a warrior, he was herding goats on the side of the road when a white man driving a Land Rover stopped and took his picture, giving him a child's book in partial payment. The bright colored pictures of children playing with toys aroused his curiosity. He wanted to know what the strange marks beneath the pictures said about the children, and from that time, he was fired with a passion to learn to read. He had pleaded with his grandfather for permission to attend the mission school at Longonot.

Sendeu finally sold a goat to pay the tuition, saying his young grandson would soon tire of the foolish notion. But Sendeu was wrong. Although Mbatyani's hunger for learning grew as books opened a wide new world for him, he always came back to the reservation and his grandfather. He could barely remember his mother and father who died so long ago, but his love for Sendeu who had sponsored his initiation as a *murrani* drew him back home. He kept a notebook in a secret place to record stories the elders told about his family and Maasai history.

At least he could be proud of his bravery during the circumcision. He had not disgraced his grandfather. When the elders held him on the cowhide altar, he had not moved a muscle or cried out under the knife, but he was glad when it was over. After the old Dorobo had finished cutting the foreskin, he knew he could celebrate with his age-mates and share in their loyalties, but he didn't love them as he loved Sendeu.

"How many cattle do you own now, grandfather?" Mbatyani knew, but he liked to hear his grandfather talk about his wealth. He hoped it would lead to other stories about his ancestors moving south along the Nile into Kenya, defeating all other tribes, terrorizing them with courage and superior strength. He liked to hear the descriptions of the magnificent lion skin headdresses, fierce war-paint, sharp iron spears, and long, painted cowhide shields.

"More than a hundred," Sendeu said, and he began to list them. He knew the name of every cow and how many calves she'd had. He even remembered the name of each frisky goat, and he named each water hole from Longonot to Naivasha.

"I believe you love your cattle more than your wives," Mbatyani teased.

"That's true. More than myself. I would give my life to protect them from a lion," Sendeu said. Then with a serious face, he added, "A man can always find another wife but cattle are a man's survival and status. It's time for you to get married and take your place in the tribe," he said. "You need sons to herd cattle."

Sendeu had once chosen a wife for Mbatyani. She was young and beautiful with a full-moon face framed by collars of bright beads. Her head was shaved and polished with oil and her forehead circled with silver bangles. She was fresh from initiation and trained to be an obedient wife. Her breasts were firm and her skin was as smooth and soft as the flanks of a gazelle. As much as Mbatyani wanted her, he knew she couldn't quiet his restlessness. When he refused, her father had married her to an old man with cattle.

"I've told you, grandfather. I don't have enough cattle to get married."

"I'm a wealthy man. That could be arranged," Sendeu said, "but you're stubborn in your bones. Going to school has made you useless."

Mbatyani knew his grandfather was right. His education had made him useless for Maasai life, but he couldn't leap from his shadowy stone age past into the space age without pain. A traditional wife would add to his conflict. He had worked at times in Narok to earn money for a bicycle, but he always came home bringing beads and cloth for his aunts. His village was home where he belonged, and he loved his beautiful people. They walked with dignity, one foot in front of the other like the crested crane, and their bodies were strong and straight with creamy skins lighter than the Bantu. He loved being with *il murran* when they plaited hair and smoothed it with ocher clay and oil. He liked to draw designs on his legs and face, and dance and leap to hunting chants. He liked the power and vigor of war dances and games of combat. But it all seemed so useless. There were no tribal wars, hunting wild game was illegal, and the government had taken their pastures for farming, pushing them farther into drought and desert county on Trust Land with the wild animals. Sometimes they were treated as much a tourist attraction as the animals. Their only chance for survival was to adapt to the modern world, but his grandfather couldn't see that.

Far away, they saw something silver shining near the horizon like a bright star, something which did not belong to the land. They arrived when the burning sun was near the top of the sky. They loosened their blankets and stood leaning on their staffs by the side of the road and gazed at what they saw. Two silver platforms built of ladders reached high into the sky. On top of each, great silver bowls were cupped like ears, listening. The bowls rotated slightly. Sendeu's keen eyes detected delicate rotations as he had often seen the ears of antelope tilt when alerted to danger. He looked beyond them but saw only a wide expanse of amber sky. He strained to hear with his ears, but he heard only the whispering of wind gathering a pocket of dust which whirled about his head, irritating his eyes.

"Perhaps," Sendeu said, "they are like the ears of elephants and leopards. Animals can hear things men cannot hear." He stood gazing at the box-like metal buildings at the base of the platforms, thinking how ugly it all was.

Mbatyani turned when he heard a familiar sound like the singing of a bee. "That's the plane that flies over our village," he said to Sendeu. He watched a small plane settle on a flat stretch of land nearby and taxi to a stop. Two men, stepping lightly as only young men walk, hurried into the building. Mbatyani was delirious with curiosity. He wanted to learn to fly a plane like that, and he wanted to learn more about the silver bowls.

When they walked away, Sendeu's turned a sad face to his grandson. "Those ones are very clever," he said, "but they do not love the earth enough to respect it. They will destroy us all."

Going home, Mbatyani insisted his grandfather lean against him, holding his arm as they walked, but as time passed, Sendeu walked more slowly and Mbatyani put his arm around him for support, almost carrying him at times. Mbatyani knew he had been too weak for the long walk and made no attempt at conversation.

"I have had a good life," Sendeu said. "I'm ready for the spirit world."

"Don't talk like that, grandfather," Mbatyani said. "I'm not ready for you to go. You're all I have."

"Promise me you will take my body to the mountain I love and let it be eaten by nature."

"I promise," Mbatyani said, "but, please, you mustn't talk like this."

"I'm at peace with the land and myself," he said, "and I've outlived my time. I'm satisfied that I've lived a life in keeping with Maasai customs. I was brave during the circumcision ceremony. I was honored for bravery during cattle raids. I have learned all the dances, history, and legends. I have not let a woman see me eat meat, and I have not used alcohol or tobacco. I have always protected the sacred earth, never hurting it more than necessary. I have not pierced the ground to plant a garden or bury the dead, and I've refused to drink from wells dug by thoughtless government workers. I've owned large herds of cattle and given many children to four wives. I have fulfilled my duty as an elder by making hard decisions for the village and have done my part in ceremonies."

Sendeu was breathless when he finished his long speech of affirmation. They didn't speak again until they reached home.

"Take me up the mountain to the big stone," Sendeu said as they came in sight of the village. Mbatyani was touched when his grandfather asked for help. His voice was humble, so different from his words of that morning. Mbatyani thought how much he must have wanted to see the silver bowls and felt no regrets for taking him.

He carried Sendeu up the steep mountain side, helped him sit on the large granite boulder at the base of the eroded crater and stood beside him, watching. Sendeu pulled his blanket tighter around his shoulders. A light breeze drifted up from the valley chilling his bare skin underneath. He turned his wizened face toward the small whirlwinds lifting flares of yellow dust. When he turned his head, his long beaded earrings touched the coarse threads of his woven blanket—a blanket the color of clay like the mixture of oil and clay that decorated his hair and forehead. He blended with the landscape as naturally as dry grass and yellow thorn. His eyes studied the uneven ridge of mountains where the Mau Escarpment outlined the Great Rift Valley, a prehistoric wound in the earth that had healed, scarred over, and now provided sparse grazing for Maasai cattle. The distant hills were shrouded in layers of blue haze, intense and mysterious. Wisps of white mist drifted among ragged peaks like smoke from fires of the god, Enkai. Mbatyani watched his grandfather's face as he sat motionless on the stone with his staff pointing skyward like a spear as he did most afternoons. He had often wondered what he thought about sitting here like a statue, but Sendeu's placid face gave no clues. He seemed at peace.

The red plaid blankets of his grandsons, the warrior herdsmen, made them visible from far across the valley. They were coming home, and it would be almost dark when cattle were settled in the thorn-brush corrals and the evening meal was finished. Mbatyani carried Sendeu down the side of the mountain, laid him on his sleeping mat, and sat beside him while he waited for one of his nieces to draw milk and blood for their evening meal.

He fed Sendeu first from the slender gourd and then drank what was left and fastened the leather cap.

The sun had disappeared behind low clouds. Soft murmurs drifted from the *manyattas* and from small groups gathered to collect firewood or prepare for the night. Mbatyani felt sad to know the old ways could not last for him. When his grandfather was gone, he would leave. He knew he could do more to help his people through education and working in the city than he could by staying home. Village people had no power. When they felt mistreated by the government, their only recourse was to kill a rare rhinoceros. There was no way for the government to prosecute as nobody would tell who killed the endangered animal.

Darkness descended suddenly. He collected his spear and blanket from his hut and joined an age-mate, Kundele, to stand guard for the night. The moon was full, peering like a voyeur over the rim of the crater. Shadows moved among the thorn-brush fences cautioning him to be alert, watchful. He spoke with Kundele only when necessary and in a low voice. Tension was in the night. The air was cold. He drew his blanket around his shoulders, wishing he could build a fire, but he didn't want Kundele to think he was weak. He paced beside the fence to relieve numbness in his bare feet. At the slightest sound or movement, he grew rigid, ready to throw his spear, but the night was slow and tedious. The fat moon, which had spread its ghostly light across the *enkang*, dropped behind the rim of the valley. He thought about Sendeu and wondered if he would feel better after a long rest.

Mbatyani began to think about daylight and the warmth of morning sun when he heard the distant hum of a small plane flying from the direction of the silver bowls. He recognized the sound; the same plane flew over the village several times each week and he thought nothing of it. He listened, unconcerned, as the plane soared over the valley, flying low.

The plane turned, losing altitude. Mbatyani stood transfixed, watching the flashing landing lights as the plane descended. In the dark, the plane seemed only a few yards away, coming directly at him. He felt Kundele grasp his arm and pull him into the open plain.

They ran blindly, not knowing where to go. Mbatyani knew he could conquer a lion or a hyena, but he was helpless before the onslaught of a plane. He tried not to scream as the plane plunged. The shadowy form swayed, flipped into a spin, and burst into flames. Like a winged eagle swooping for its prey, the plane touched the ground at the edge of the corral, scooping up cattle and goats, splintering the thorn-brush fence, setting it on fire.

Mbatyani and Kundele raced back to save cattle. One side of the dry bush corral was crackling with flames. The acrid odor of burning thorn choked him. The fire spread fast. He held his breath trying not to breathe smoke. Heat seared his cheeks. Cows bawled and goats bleated, tumbling over each other trying to get out. He picked up a calf and carried it outside the ring of fire, taking a deep breath as he did so. The calf's mother was too wounded to save.

The place came alive with people, running about wildly, getting in their way of saving livestock, wailing for their lost wealth. The cattle seemed to have lost directions and refused to be driven by their panicked owners through the narrow gate, away from the great glare of flames. Mbatyani thought of Sendeu's words, "Those ones are very clever, but they do not love the earth enough to respect it. They will destroy us all."

He raced to Sendeu's hut to wake him. Sendeu was lying on his side, his knees drawn up, rigid to his touch. Mbatyani lit a candle, placing it on the mat near Sendeu's face and saw that his eyes were glazed with the unseeing stare of death; he must have been dead for several hours. Mbatyani lay beside him on the mat, crying, but he was glad Sendeu had not seen the destruction of his cattle, the animals he knew by name and would have given his life to save.

Morning dawned clear with only a suggestion of mist on the crater. Uniformed officers came in vans and trucks to take away the charred bodies of the men who had been inside the plane. They loaded broken and twisted metal on trucks. They also brought district officers with them who stayed to talk with elders about payment for damages. Mbatyani, together with Kundele and his grandfather's wives, carried Sendeu to the large stone where he loved to sit looking out over the valley and left his body there to be eaten by nature. Mbatyani knew he would not want them to pierce the earth for his sake.

The next morning, Mbatyani dressed in Western clothes, gathered his notebook and a few possessions into a woven basket, got on his bicycle, and rode toward Nairobi to look for work. He didn't want the warriors, *il murran*, to see the tears. He didn't want to say goodbye to anyone, and he didn't know when he would be coming back.

That Last Small Thing

Some sane day, not too bright and not too stormy
I shall be gone, and you may whistle for me.
Edna St. Vincent Millay

Lois hummed as she packed her battered blue suitcase. She and Jensen had lived in the village ever since they'd arrived in Kenya where he worked with World Missions as an agricultural specialist. At last they were going to spend a week in Nairobi. While Jensen attended meetings, she planned to visit the game park outside the city, rummage through little boutiques, maybe buy a tie-dyed dress. Mostly, she hoped Jensen could relax and get his life back in balance, then maybe he wouldn't work so hard or be so irritable. She feared for their marriage or that he might become abusive; the return ticket back home to St. Paul, hidden way among her clothes, gave her a small feeling of security on days when she felt she could stay no longer.

Lois remembered the time she and Jensen had driven to the nearest town for shopping. Trying to meet Jensen's rigid time schedule, they separated, agreeing to meet at one o'clock in front of the meat market. Because her watch stopped, she was late and he had already gone home. She rode home in a *matatu*, one of those little covered trucks, squeezed among sweaty vendors carrying live chickens and baskets of vegetables. She felt humiliated and furious about his abandoning her. Back in St.

Paul she'd had a job, her own money, a car to go and come as she pleased. Her dependency frightened her. The *matatu* let her off at least a mile from home. She walked the dusty road in twilight to find Jensen working on records in his bedroom. He looked up, unconcerned.

"You weren't on time," he said. "I was there exactly at one." He looked at his watch.

She felt a choking anger she had not known before. "My watch stopped," she said.

"That's no excuse." His voice was hard. "The world's in the mess it's in because people don't do things at the proper time." His eyes narrowed. "You must learn to be on time." He returned to his work, dismissing her.

Lois resented being treated like a child, but looking at him sitting in the straight wooden chair, the light of the kerosene lamp shining on his blond hair, and as handsome as the day she married him, a tenderness filtered through her anger. She wished they could have fun, holidays, adventures, weekend trips like they'd had back in Minnesota, but he was like a different person—tense, self-centered, unapproachable.

She heard the rustle of his packing in the next room, the room he now called his. In the scarred mirror above the home-made dressing table, she smoothed on lip gloss which exaggerated her wide mouth, ran a comb through her straight brown hair, and wished she didn't have such a big nose. She tucked an extra pair of hose among the lingerie and remembered to include black patent pumps. She folded one good dress she had brought all the way from St. Paul having no idea it would go to waste in the African bush.

Nobody had told her what to expect before she came to live in the stone mission house on the edge of the village. Her boss wouldn't give her the day off when Jensen had his job orientation, and Jensen hadn't shared what he had learned; he was not a verbal person. The only advice she'd had was from Mrs. Watson, a missionary's wife who had lived in the bush for twenty years and who had been assigned to meet them at the airport.

"Be careful," she had warned while Jensen collected their luggage. "There's something about the frustrations men experience out here that exaggerates whatever problems they bring with them."

At the time Lois had smiled, puzzled by the woman's earnestness.

Now she understood, and her loss of confidence frightened her. She often felt lonely, confused, troubled over small decisions. Her problem at the moment was deciding what to wear on the long, dusty trip to Nairobi. She sorted through her wardrobe in the big hall closet, pushing the garments aside, conscious of the scrape of hangers on the rusty metal pole. She finally decided on a long-sleeved blouse to protect her arms from mosquitoes and a denim skirt with silver buckles. Her fingers trembled as she stood by the window trying to button her blouse. Excitement? Fear? She couldn't decide.

Outside, in the small ravine behind the house, African women in bright head-cloths and flowered dresses washed clothes in the muddy stream as they had done every day as long as she had lived there. On lonely days, she had stood at the open window, lost in time, her scuffed fingers holding back the dusty curtain, her hair ruffled by the constant breeze circulating through the old house.

She watched women spread clothes on the grass to dry, or lift heavy tubs of wet laundry to their heads balancing them with both hands, arms uplifted, forming stylized silhouettes against the landscape as they trudged uphill. Sometimes she envied their simple, uncluttered lives; at other times she was overcome with pity that tightened her throat and stung her eyes. They were country women, bought and married for a price, and at the mercy of husbands. Women told her some men felt obliged to beat their wives to make them obedient, but this she had not seen.

There were times when she could identify with these women and their burden of work when she washed clothes in wooden tubs behind the house and hung them on a line in the kitchen to dry. She couldn't understand the extent of their poverty and their patient acceptance of verbal or physical abuse.

She stood at the stove stirring stew for dinner thinking about the women when Jensen stormed into the house, his face twisted in anger, the dimple in his chin twitching as it always did when he was upset. He paced until she called him to eat. She had made his favorite stew that afternoon and had gone to the local market to get tomatoes. The vendors always had tomatoes, but that day they had only greens, *sukumu wiki*, onions, and mangoes. She wanted to have something he liked for dinner as a special treat; she knew the meeting with the village elders wouldn't be easy.

"What's this garbage?" Jensen yelled when she set the plate before him. His lips curled.

"I tried to make your favorite stew..." she said, but he cut her off before she could finish.

"Then why didn't you make it right!" His face was contorted.

A paralyzing fear rose within her like a bad dream, her eyes wide and disbelieving. "There were no tomatoes in the market."

"There are always tomatoes in the market," he yelled, towering over her.

He is being irrational, she thought. He knows how hard it is to find a variety of vegetables in the country markets.

Lois rose, escaping to her bedroom, but as she turned, Jensen swung at her. She dodged; his fist crashed into the wooden frame around the kitchen door. Back in St. Paul he had been unpleasant about little things, like her habit of chewing gum or leaving her toothbrush out of its holder, but he had never threatened to strike her.

She closed her bedroom door and locked it. Lying curled on the bed, straining to hold back tears, she tried to imagine what had made him lose control. She saw village leaders sitting in a group making long, tiresome speeches in a language Jensen didn't know, using precious time when they could have been working. She imagined Jensen's plans rejected for tribal reasons, for local customs he didn't understand. She understood how he must feel, but she could not excuse his behavior. Frightened and alone, she lay wondering if Jensen had the understanding or patience to negotiate with authoritarian elders.

She expected Jensen to apologize for striking out at her, but neither of them ever mentioned the incident. Although she tried to forgive his silence, fear and caution lingered. She recalled Mrs. Watson's anxious face and her words, "Be careful. There's something about the frustrations..."

Lois slipped into her leather sandals and drew the denim skirt over her head. As she smoothed the skirt over her hips, the mirror picked up reflections from the roof of the church on the hill near the compound. She looked out the window again and thought of the church as an example of Jensen's frustrations. It would be a Catholic church when it was finished but had been nothing but a shell since they arrived. The aluminum roof, shaped like a pyramid, glistened like polished silver in morning sun. The rough walls of multicolored stones gave the building an ambiance of permanence. Drawn by its beauty, Lois had walked through the church on one of her many lonely wanderings. She found nothing inside but broken mortar and scattered stones on bare ground where lizards skittered searching for insects. When she asked the village headman about the church, he shrugged and said the priest had run out of money. It would be finished, he said, maybe next year. But almost a year had passed and no work was done. Village people brought their goats and skinny cows to graze while they sat in the dust looking at the church—and waited.

She knew the waiting upset Jensen most. He wasn't satisfied to let things happen. He wanted to make them happen. Farmers were willing to use profits to improve their farms, but today they wanted to buy another wife. Yes, they would use fertilizer, but there was no hurry; their grandfathers had not used it, and they had been wise men. Crop rotation was a good thing, but their fathers had not rotated crops. Maybe next year. The slow and easy flow of living was alien to Jensen's mind. He wanted to set a precise time for doing things and follow a schedule. Why should it take a week to plant a small field of maize when the job could be done in two days?

At night she lay awake planning how she could help him adjust, thinking they really should go home. She'd watched him grow hostile, intolerant, self-righteous, determined to bend his small world to accomplish what he had set out to do — improve African farming, feed more people, improve living conditions. His intentions were good, but he was going about it all wrong, even Lois could see that. But Jensen placed little value on her judgment.

She heard the latch on Jensen's suitcase click shut and knew he was ready to go. Although they slept together on the big wooden bed in the corner of her bedroom, Jensen kept all his personal things in a separate room, increasingly bound to ritual and order, meticulous about small things. Even at home in Minnesota, he hadn't liked things out of place, but here, order had become an obsession. Lois hoped the week in Nairobi would help him relax and flow with time instead of trying to master it.

She made a mental inventory of things she had packed: lingerie, sandals, dress shoes, walking shoes, sweaters, a raincoat, cosmetics, passport, malaria pills, travelers' checks, and, oh yes, the large package of sugar-free gum she had brought from home. She had rationed it carefully—a small piece at a time. When Jensen was away, she sometimes chewed gum to relieve tension and loneliness. If she forgot she had gum in her mouth when he returned, his disgusted looks reminded her to get rid of it. She resented Jensen's attitude, angry that he didn't allow her one small weakness when he had so many of his own. He wanted her to be perfect, his kind of perfect.

She looked beneath the layers of folded sweaters on the closet shelf; the package of gum was not where she remembered hiding it. She searched through her lingerie drawer, the desk drawers filled with writing paper and sewing things, her cosmetic drawer. She was rummaging through an old suitcase when she saw a shadow at the door. She looked up. Jensen was watching her, leaning on the door, hands in the pockets of his bush jeans.

"About ready to go?" he asked.

"Almost."

"What are you looking for?"

"The sugar-free gum I brought from home. I must have misplaced it."

Jensen chuckled, his blue eyes crinkled at the corners. Lois caught her breath; he was so good looking when he laughed, and she had not seen him laugh much lately. Lord, how she wanted him to be happy!

"So that's why you're digging in that suitcase like a woodchuck," he said.

"Have you seen it?" Lois asked, brave now that he wasn't angry.

"No, I haven't."

"Well, that's all right. I can buy more when we get to Nairobi, but it might not be sugar-free."

"Don't you dare!" Jensen said, his voice low and threatening. "Chewing gum is a disgusting habit. I threw it away."

Lois stared at him. The shock of his words gave her chills that spread through her body radiating to her fingertips.

"How could you!" she said, her voice cold and even. "It belonged to me."

"You're revolting when you chew gum," he said. His face contorted with distaste.

Lois stood beside her packed suitcase, her arms hanging limp at her sides. She stared at him speechless, unbelieving. She knew she wasn't beautiful, but he had called her revolting, and he had thrown away a special thing that gave her a little comfort, a secret thing she could call her own. Any feeling she had for him drained away. She didn't hate him, but she didn't love him either. The blond hair matted to his forehead and his square jaw were no longer handsome. The blue eyes which once sent throbbing rhythms of desire through her body looked faded and pale. He could have been an ordinary man anywhere who meant nothing, a stranger, perhaps. She stared, puzzled by the revelation.

He turned away. "I'll be outside when you're ready," he said.

She heard his heavy footsteps as he carried suitcases, coolers, and boxes out to the van. The metal front door shut with a familiar bang that echoed through the house; the car door closed with a metallic thud. She knew he wouldn't be back to help carry her bags.

Trembling, Lois threw more clothes into her suitcase, pounded it shut and latched it with determination. She checked her traveling purse again for passport, health records, credit cards, travelers' checks—they were all there. She found the other half of her round-trip ticket hidden behind her sweaters and tucked it into the inside pocket of her purse, zipping it shut.

"It's silly," she thought, "how a package of gum can make me feel so dead!" She knew what happened had nothing to do with gum. It was that last small thing telling her what she had to do.

She glanced for the last time at the familiar scene of women washing clothes in the muddy stream, children playing beside their mothers, clothes spread on the grass to dry.

In her mind something clicked as if she had opened a shutter and photographed a picture she wanted to keep forever. "We're much alike," she said aloud. "But there's one big difference. I can leave."

She wouldn't mention the gum again. During the long ride, she would be pleasant and obedient, "a wife to pattern by." Even after she was safe in Nairobi, she wouldn't tell Jensen her plans until it was too late for him to interfere.

She gathered up her luggage and, struggling under the weight, walked out of the house without looking back, without locking the door, out to the dusty van where Jensen waited, beeping the horn impatiently.

NIGHT FLIGHT

Linda woke to the sound of a gunshot. Still half asleep, she reached across the bed to wake John, then remembered he was away on a State Department assignment. She sat up, rigid, tense, listening. She was alone in the big house. Was somebody trying to break in? Or was John coming home early?

"John? Is that you?" she called.

Silence.

"Who's there?" she called again, forcing her voice.

No answer, only night sounds: the rustle of a lizards climbing vines near her window and the crackle of insects.

Her head throbbed. She felt faint. Images passed before her eyes as in a dream, but she knew she was awake. She saw a cinder block storage shed with a corrugated tin roof, broken bicycles leaning against a baobab tree, clumps of twisted trees and scrub bushes, and the distinct sound of a waterfall. Breathing in shallow gasps, she groped in the dark for the light switch on her bedside lamp, fumbling at the chain; it was four o'clock in the morning. She sat on the side of the bed, her bare feet cold against the tile floor.

"My God!" she whispered. "Something has happened to John."

John had been assigned to investigate the deaths of two Americans killed in Zimbabwe near Victoria Falls—two traveling university students ambushed in one of those magnificent ravines. The government of Zimbabwe provided little information. John was sent to sort out the details. Linda remembered all the times she had felt deserted when she was not allowed to travel with John, but this was considered a "safe" assignment. Staying alone in a government guest house in Zambia on the outskirts of Lusaka, she felt even more deserted and was anxious to go home.

Linda knew how John felt about her "waking dreams." Five years of marriage to a man on secret missions who couldn't talk about his work and who was away from home for weeks, sometimes months at a time, had created awkwardness and misunderstanding. The stress and loneliness had excited Linda into a series of dreams like those plaguing her sleep when she was a child. She'd lost her engagement ring and found it when, in a dream, she saw it among sweaters in a dresser drawer. She'd dreamed John's mother called from Minneapolis to break the news his father was in surgery, and she had predicted precisely some of the details. There also had been premonitions about things of little consequence, but when she told John about them, he'd laughed.

"You're so silly," he said. "My Kitten sure has an active imagination." He always called her Kitten when he wasn't serious.

"I wish I could make you believe me," Linda sighed.

They had not talked about the subject again, but her dreams persisted with vividness and regularity. She remembered the heavy burden of guilt she felt for not warning John's best friend about an automobile accident which hospitalized him causing great expense and suffering. There were times when she wanted so much to share her dreams with John or talk with close friends, but an inner voice warned her. People who didn't understand such things might think her superstitious or a little crazy.

A conversation with John drove her to complete secrecy.

She was sitting in an easy chair one evening thinking about her dreams, nervously twisting strands of her long brown hair waiting for John to emerge from behind layers of newspaper. Finally, she had nudged his arm.

"John, I've had several dreams lately telling me things that are going to happen." She paused, waiting for him to respond. "I believe God gave me this gift, and I should use it to help people."

The crackle of newspaper filled the silent space between them as he crushed the newsprint into his lap. His dark eyes grew wide behind horn-rimmed glasses. "For God's sake, Linda," he exploded. "Don't be a freak!"

Linda stared at her hands clasped in her lap, the knuckles white against her dark skirt. His attitude surprised and frightened her. She tried to excuse him by thinking there are always secret things husbands and wives don't know about each other or that he must be worried about something at work. After that, she had tried to block out dreams and entered a long dry period, feeling empty, depressed, alienated from John.

The sound of the gun had come so forcefully she couldn't ignore it. She would never forgive herself if she took no action. But how? Telling the truth would be madness. She could imagine the amused look on the deputy administrator's face if she said, "In my dream, I heard a gunshot . . ."

Linda lay alone in the big double bed, frustrated by helplessness. Every muscle was tensed for action. Her eyes probed the darkness; her ears were tuned to record the slightest sound. At daybreak, she heard the first feeble chirps of birds, and then the rhythmic throbbing of drums drifting across the field from Kaunda Square where village people had settled. Standing in front of wide French doors opening upon a path leading to a thatched gazebo, she watched a shy mongoose slink along the base of a low stone wall hunting for cobra. She thought about how both people and animals prey upon each other, and she could wait no longer.

Thumbing through the frayed pages of her address book, she dialed the number of the United States Embassy. The Embassy connection buzzed as it switched to the home number of the officer on night duty. She felt relieved when she recognized the man's voice. His "Hello" was strident and heavy with sleep.

"Mr. Herbert? This is Linda Watson."

"Yes," he said. "What's wrong?"

"I have information that John may be in danger."

"How can I help you?"

"Can you investigate?"

"I'll need the details and where you got your information," he said, suddenly awake. "Give me time to write everything down."

"I can't tell you the source of my information right now, but please check. And hurry!"

There was a long pause. "I've known you and John for seven years, Linda," Mr. Herbert said. "I know you wouldn't call except in an emergency, but I need reliable facts."

"Tell them," Linda continued, "to look for John in a cinder-block shed or a warehouse with a rusting tin roof."

Mr. Herbert hesitated. "That might help, but there may be many buildings like that where he's working."

"This one is outside the city near Victoria Falls at a point where two roads converge into a Y," she said, wishing he could see the pictures she had seen. "Two broken bicycles are parked beside a large baobab tree which is on the right near the entrance." She paused, realizing she had said almost enough to destroy credibility. "And Mr. Herbert," she added, trying to disguise the urgency she felt. "Please don't tell anyone I told you unless you have to."

"If you could tell me where you got the details, I'd have more to work with."

"Please!" Linda said. "I can't tell you."

"All right." He sighed. "I'll see what I can do."

Day stretched into night. Instead of reading in the study, she surprised Ndopu, the house servant, by helping him clean the patio. She walked around the guest house, and finding a long-neglected rose garden, began transplanting, pruning, and watering thorny stalks which offered no promise of roses in that dry season. She ate dinner alone by candlelight in the cavernous dining room, conscious of Ndopu's searching gaze.

In reading about tribal rituals and ceremonies before coming to Zambia, she had learned that priests and diviners depend upon visions and dreams for guidance. She felt Ndopu might understand if she told him about the dream. When their eyes met, she opened her mouth to tell him but changed her mind; there was no way he could help. She withdrew into her private shell of silence. He tiptoed in and out of the room respecting her mood.

All next day she watched the driveway expecting a messenger to arrive telling her John had been shot. She waited all evening by the telephone. When no news came, a calm settled over her, a resignation, as if waiting for the inevitable. There was still no question in her mind, and though she *knew*, she was determined not to call the Embassy again. If officials had bad news, they'd call her, and she didn't want to embarrass John.

Almost a week later, her daily routine was interrupted by the sound of his rented Peugeot jolting up the graveled driveway. Rushing to the door, she saw John swinging up the front steps wearing a boyish grin, his left arm in a sling. At the doorway, his right arm lifted her off her feet, swung her around; he planted a kiss on her forehead.

"Hi, Kitten," he said, laughing. "It's good to be home."

"I was worried!" Linda's voice was choked with emotion. John looked eager, relaxed, happy. Linda's heart skipped a beat; his affectionate hug brought back the excitement of getting to know him, of the early days of their marriage, and reminded her how much she still cared.

"No need to worry," he said lightly, but he flinched when she touched his bandaged arm.

"What's wrong?" She reached out to him but he pulled away.

"I'll tell you later," he said.

Tossing his briefcase on the table, he opened it with one hand and pulled out plane tickets. "The State Department is calling us home. We're leaving tonight, and that's not a minute too soon for me." He squinted at the dim carbon markings on his ticket. "Flight 176."

"That doesn't give us much time."

"When you travel with me," he said, "you travel light and move on short notice."

"But Ndopu hasn't finished the laundry."

He ignored her protest. "With this bad arm, I'll need a lot of help. Let's get busy."

The Embassy vehicle arrived after dark. An armed military aide in civilian clothes sat beside a sour-faced African driver. Linda and John held hands in the back seat, their thighs touching when the vehicle bounced over potholes. The military aide spoke only when necessary, and the driver responded with grunts and nods. The atmosphere was tense, and, Linda thought, a little melodramatic.

The aide escorted them through the security check, but when they were finally settled in the waiting area beside the boarding gate, Linda turned to John. "All right," she said. "It's time you told me what happened at Victoria Falls."

"I'll tell you when we're out of the country."

"I want to know now," Linda insisted. "I'm your wife, remember?"

"Someone might overhear us," he said, looking about. He was obviously afraid of something.

"If you don't tell me, I'll worry more."

He led her away from other passengers and began, his voice almost a whisper. "I was assigned to examine the site of the ambush," John began. He paused to take a deep breath. "My driver was released, but I was captured by members of the African National Congress. The ANC has a headquarters just over the border into Zimbabwe used for organizing resistance in South Africa. My captors were convinced I was a mercenary working for the South African government."

"But how did you get shot? What did they do to you?"

"Do?" John echoed. "They stripped me and held me captive in an old warehouse for three days under almost continuous interrogation. The situation got ugly. A gun-happy guard shot me in the arm trying to get me to confess to being a South African spy. My escape was a miracle, like something out of a mystery novel. Some anonymous caller tipped off the U.S. Embassy which got help from Zambian troops. Soldiers surprised them and we . . . ."

Outside on the runway a 747 revved for take-off, its great motors drowning out details of his release. Through a thick veil of sound his words came faint and far away like an echo chopped to distortion by erratic wind. The motor's monotonous drone enclosed her in its hypnotic rhythm, and she felt herself vibrating on a frequency as delicate as an uneven heartbeat. The sensation grew intense, penetrating. Her head throbbed. Then the vision came. She felt pressure at the back of her neck, a numbness, a paralyzing chill. Disjointed images of wreckage lay scattered across the flat, sun-burned plains, among twisted acacia trees, a broken fuselage, fragments of luggage and shattered bodies. . .

Linda shuddered and shifted in her seat, screaming ,"No! No!"

"Linda, what's wrong?" John cried, trying to put his arm around her. "I'm sorry I upset you. I shouldn't have told you."

"It's not that," Linda cried. "I saw a plane crash . . . scattered wreckage . . . I saw it. We mustn't get on that plane!"

People around them began to stare. John knelt beside her, grasping her hands in his large calloused ones and looked into her face. He saw an earnestness that frightened him, but his voice was quiet and calm. "You're getting hysterical, Linda. Get hold of yourself."

Linda pointed to the runway. "One of those planes will crash tonight," she insisted.

John stood up and turned away. He looked around as if wondering what to do.

"I felt it. I saw it! I know. Please believe me," Linda begged.

"But it won't be our plane, Kitten," John said, humoring her, "It will be okay. Okay!".

"We don't know that," she said.

"You're talking nonsense," John snapped. "Now, stop it!" He shook her by the shoulder.

Cold anger replaced despair. "Will you believe me if I tell you I was the anonymous caller that saved your life?"

John stared at her. "I don't believe it."

"Check with Mr. Herbert." She held her chin high. "I called him for help."

John's face drained of color. He slumped in the seat beside her and watched passengers file out to board the waiting planes. She could see he was worried about staying in the airport overnight. She knew the Embassy wanted him out of the country on that night flight.

"All right, Kitten," he said. "We'll try to reschedule our flights," but knowing him, she suspected he was thinking "Damn! What nonsense! Of all the women I could have married, why did I have to marry such a dingbat," and then he would feel guilty for thinking of her that way.

They sat in the waiting room all night. Linda dozed, but John paced. She knew his mind was racing with all the problems that would result. Their luggage was already on the plane. A car would be waiting at Dulles Airport. He might not be able to transfer the tickets. She imagined that next morning, while negotiating with airlines for a "next flight out," he would buy a Zambian Times, as he always did, and a headline would catch his eye. He'd pick up the paper, stare at it, and glance through the lead paragraph. She wondered what he would say when the paper reported United Airlines had lost radio contact with flight 176 somewhere over Sudan. *Helicopters were searching the area. . . Airline officials were interviewing employees and checking passenger lists. . . Terrorists activity was suspected.*

Why Francis Kicked the Telephone

Francis Mataba stood in a long line waiting to use a telephone booth in front of the postoffice at Nakuru, Kenya. He was tall, thin and in his early twenties. He slumped, looking down at his frayed canvas shoes and wondered how much longer he could survive without work. He wore his only suit of clothes: a faded blue shirt and a pair of worn gray trousers. By contrast, the men who interviewed him wore dark business suits and seemed interested only in their own self-importance. They bustled about their offices smiling and speaking with friends, flirting with secretaries, shuffling piles of papers which seemed to produce no results, and socialized on telephones. They appeared immensely satisfied with themselves—or so it seemed to Francis.

Sometimes they told him to leave his name and they would get in touch, but they never asked where he could be reached. Their clipped voices and cool manners discouraged Francis from volunteering the information. Some people told him to come back next April or June when they might be hiring, but they didn't bother to ask his name. Francis knew he was only one of many faceless job-seekers who plagued their offices and who became an annoyance like the flies they swatted. They were eager to get rid of him as quickly as possible and with the least possible conflict. He found their attitudes humiliating.

His most recent contact was with a paper company in need

of a storeroom worker. He was willing to take any available job even though he knew his Form IV education made him eligible to do more than storeroom work. The buxom secretary standing between him and a company interview said they were looking for somebody with experience. He was not at all sure how much experience one needed to sort boxes and put them on shelves which was mainly what the job was about. The secretary said she would speak to the personnel manager, Mr. Maina, just in case, but Francis would have to call today between ten o'clock and noon to make an appointment. "No, don't come in," she had said. "Just call."

Francis felt in his pocket for the four shillings he had been saving for important occasions such as this. He fingered the silver coins with his thumb and forefinger, separating them one by one, visualizing them in his mind. When these were gone, he didn't know where he would get more. He'd been living on the outside of town in a hut with his cousin's cousin, and it was obvious the man's wife was tired of having him around. Lately, she had cooked at odd times, and when he came home after a long day of job hunting so hungry he felt he had a hole in his stomach, she said there was nothing to eat.

Francis had borrowed shillings from everybody he knew and some people he didn't know, and he could think of nothing more to do except beg. As he stood, restless in the long line, it occurred to him that he was least qualified to be a beggar. He wasn't missing fingers or toes, he didn't have twisted limbs, he wasn't blind and couldn't pretend to be, and he didn't look sick or insane. If he sat on the street with his begging bowl, people would look at him with suspicion and those who knew him would wonder why an able-bodied Form IV graduate wasn't out looking for work. Besides, he was a proud man. He would rather steal than beg.

He counted the people in the line in front of him—eight, five men and three women. He studied the other three telephone booths and thought about changing lines, but they were also long. He would gain nothing there. He glanced at the clock through the open door of the postoffice and felt a moment of panic. It was almost noon; the offices would be closing and wouldn't open again until 2:00 p.m. Then he remembered the clock was not in operation and had not been since he came to Nakuru. He raised his left wrist to look at his watch, a reflex action which made him feel more depressed. He wished he had not been forced to sell his watch to get food. He looked again at the telephone booth ahead of him and saw the man in the booth was not talking but was leaning against the wall waiting for a call. A man in a tan jacket behind Francis paced in a circle.

"What's going on up there?" the man yelled when he saw no action in the booth. A tall man in front of Francis said with disgust, "He's one of those reverse callers."

Francis knew what that meant. The man had used one shilling, giving him three minutes to talk, to call a friend in a public office. Then he left the pay phone number for his friend to call back so they could visit while people waited. He might talk for an hour. Francis studied the man standing with crossed legs in the door of the booth. He was a morose man with a thin face, dressed in dirty jeans and a striped cotton T-shirt. When the phone rang, he snatched the receiver and jumped to attention. From his expression of excitement and animated pleasure, Francis decided it would be a long social call. He checked the time with the man in the tan jacket—almost eleven—and decided to move over to the next phone.

Only four people were in front of him now as the callers had been more considerate. With some luck, he would be able to make his call before the offices closed for lunch. He stood directly behind a young woman wearing a black flowered dress of some shiny material and overpowering perfume. He felt nauseated from hunger and the unfamiliar odor and studied the activities around him to pass time.

Two Maasai men lounged beside a fire hydrant near the street corner watching the rush of traffic. They had discarded their bright *shukas* for western clothes to come into town and had removed their beaded earrings, the loops of their stretched earlobes almost touching their shoulders. Even from a distance, Francis could see the threadbare sleeves of their jackets, the worn baggy trousers, the run-over shoes. They had left their spears in the village but both carried *irinkan*, powerful hardwood clubs with knot-hole heads worn smooth. They stroked their clubs almost affectionately, paced, and glanced about with dark hostile eyes. If Francis had not known how embarrassed and afraid they were, he would have thought they were looking for trouble. He sensed their uneasiness from his own rural past remembering his first visit to Nakuru.

It was at the end of primary school when he had come into town to bring his mother to the hospital. All his relatives said she had malaria, but he had learned in his health class that many things cause fevers. For days his mother had been treated by the village medicine man. When she failed to recover, Francis borrowed money to pay for a *matutu* because she was too weak to walk. He still remembered his confusion and panic when they arrived in the market place where all *matatus* load and unload. People pushed and shoved, hawkers called their wares, vehicles roared, honked, and spewed dust on his sick mother. Several times, he had to pull her out of oncoming traffic to keep her from being killed. Everything was confusing—so different from the quiet, open country. He had wanted to strike out at the rude, uncaring people. He knew fear was behind the hostility he felt on that visit, and he saw it now in the faces of the Maasai trying to look "at home" among the frightening roar of automobiles, the rush of people, and the black smoke and pollution of trucks.

The woman in front of Francis moved forward, and he moved with her. It was an automatic response as he had by now focused his attention on the shoe shine man across the street. The little barefoot man invited passing people to take a seat in the blocky homemade chair he had made from discarded lumber, still unpainted and gray from weathering. He couldn't hear what the man said, but he could imagine the flow of stock phrases he had heard so many times. "Please, sir. Shoe shine? Take a look at your shoes. You need it! I give you good price. Sit here. Sit here!"

Francis watched the man gesture, spreading his arms in a swinging movement toward the chair, his palms up. I could do that, he thought. I could go into business for myself. But Francis knew he would need several hundred shillings to invest in a shoe shine kit, a variety of polishes, and a chair. He felt into his pocket again for the four shillings and knew the time wasn't right to become a businessman. He felt relief when a man in a dark business suit sat in the homemade chair, read his newspaper, and waited while the little man made a fuss over him, polishing his shoes with a flourish.

The woman ahead of Francis moved up again and Francis followed. He was only two people away from the telephone booth. He relaxed a little, hoping to make his phone call before noon. He had to keep hoping because hope was all he had. To keep from working himself into a panic or falling into depression, he tried to distract himself by watching sales people on either side of the shoe shine man selling curios to tourists. Men sold a variety of sisal baskets, beaded bracelets, wood carvings or masks which bore little resemblance to those used in tribal rituals. Some sold Maasai heads carved with headbands which Maasai men didn't wear. Others squatted beneath the jacaranda trees beside a collection of clay vases, bowls, and candlesticks decorated with designs only tourists bought. Francis wondered how much money they made by selling on the street as not many tourists came to Nakuru. Two older men sold such things as hand-cut terry cloth or carpet inner-soles for shoes, frying pans hammered by hand from scrap metal, chipati boards for rolling wheat bread, and other items Africans might buy. He wondered if they did any better. Francis thought he might like to sell on the street, but he knew salesmen didn't craft their wares; they had to have contacts and pay commissions to craftsmen. Francis had no such contacts and no capital to get started.

Only the woman was between him and the phone booth now. He directed his attention to the man inside the booth and wished he would stop talking. He wondered why people felt the need to talk so much. Then he watched the woman insert her shilling in the coin slot and dial the number. She turned to Francis looking disappointed. "I just lost my shilling," she said. "The box is full of coins." She grimaced. "We'll have to find another phone." She walked away down the street without making her call.

Francis felt a sinking sensation in his stomach. If he had to wait in another line, he wouldn't get his call through before noon. Then at two o'clock he would have to start over. There was something about life terribly unfair. Other people found work. Other people used telephones. Other people. . .

He noticed the phone to his right where the man had made the reverse call still had a long line. The other two were now available. He had been so busy watching people across the street he hadn't noticed they were free. He moved to the phone on the left, dropped one shilling in the slot and dialed. He felt a sense of elation when the call went through. He heard a woman's voice say the name of the company. He asked to speak to Mr. Maina. "I'll see if he is in," the voice said. He listened to a long silence, then the phone went dead. He had lost his shilling, but he still had three more. He didn't understand why some telephones cut off in the middle of a conversation, but he knew such things happen.

He moved to the next booth to try again. He dropped another shilling into the slot and dialed. The phone made a buzzing, grinding noise and clicked off. Francis wanted to scream. He knew the box was also full of coins and would take no more. He pushed the coin return button and nothing happened; he had lost a second shilling. Now he had only two. He pushed frantically at the coin return, but it refused to give up his precious shilling. He banged on the telephone box feeling the wall behind it vibrate. He swallowed a lump in his throat and feared he was going to cry. He was determined not to cry before all those people waiting to call, but he burned with a terrible rage.

He banged at the coin return with his fist. With both hands, he pounded on the telephone box. He opened the door of the booth, and raising his long right leg, he kicked it again and again. Then he groaned with pain and held his foot, bouncing up and down like a baboon. He noticed a group had gathered outside the booth to watch. And they were laughing at him. One man wasn't laughing; he looked angry. He took a small notebook out of his pocket and said to Francis with authority, "Tell me your name."

"Why do you want to know my name?" Francis asked, still in the heat of frustration. He noted the man was forty, perhaps fifty, and had a balding forehead which glistened in the sun. He was a slender man, very neat in dark brown trousers and a tan sport jacket. His clothes looked expensive. Francis considered the possibility he might be somebody important. Something told him to watch his language. He wanted to scream at the man, curse him, tell him to go away, but he didn't dare.

"Don't you know you can be taken to court for destruction of property?" the man said.

Francis nodded.

"This property belongs to the telephone company," the man continued, but Francis wanted to say he didn't care.

"The telephone company should make telephones that work." Francis cried angrily. "I've been waiting in a line all morning to make a business call. When I finally reach the phone, it is out of order." Francis puffed his cheeks. The whites of his eyes were bloodshot with unshed tears.

"But kicking the phone will do no good, young man."

"It made me feel better. And besides, what business is it of yours?"

"The telephone company is my business," the man said. "I'm Mr. Njoroge, manager of this branch. I was watching you from across the street. Our office is over that bank." He pointed to a modern building housing the Bank of Kenya. One of the wide glass windows on the second floor had "Telephone Exchange" printed in small gold letters.

"My desk is in front of the window. It's part of my job to watch these telephones to make certain citizens do not destroy company property."

Francis felt sick. Some people had all bad luck, and he was one of those people. He couldn't imagine how he would get himself out of this predicament. He had only two shillings in his pocket. He couldn't pay a fine, and he couldn't afford to go to jail. How would he ever find work?

"I'm sorry, *bwana*," he said, staring at the pavement. He

wiped his forehead with the palm of his hand as if trying to wipe away anger. He felt calmer now and his voice was more controlled. He decided he must speak his mind; he had nothing to lose.

"I'm an honest man," he said, "trying to find honest work. For months I've gone from place to place. I don't want to be a criminal and I don't want to beg. I want to work, but I'm one of the thousands of faceless people looking for employment. The paper company told me to call today between ten o'clock and noon. When someone tells me to call at a certain time, that is the time I will call. I like to do things on time. I may have lost this job because of your telephones."

"Why didn't you go to the company office rather than call?" Mr. Njoroge asked, returning his pen and notebook to his coat pocket.

"The secretary said, 'Don't come. Just call.' I was there yesterday and I was told to call today. When a company tells me to do something, I expect to do it. Not tomorrow or next week, but today between ten o'clock and noon." Francis felt himself getting worked up again, but he tried to modulate his voice. "I have been very patient. I needed to make a business call, and I was depending upon your telephones, but they failed me."

Mr. Njoroge gazed at Francis critically, then he looked amused. "You are an unusual young man," he said. "Come upstairs with me and use the telephone in my office."

The lingering crowd stared at Francis as he followed Mr. Njoroge across the street and up the stairs. Francis felt himself trembling. He couldn't imagine what terrible thing might happen to him next. Mr. Njoroge took him through a door into a large office with carpets on the floor and motioned for him to sit in a chair beside a polished desk. He pointed to the white phone on the corner of his desk and said, "You are free to make your call."

Francis dialed the number with trembling fingers. Mr. Njoroge pretended to be busy, but Francis knew he was listening—and watching. That made him even more nervous. When the secretary answered the phone, Francis told her his name and asked for Mr. Maina, reminding her that she had told him to call for an interview.

"He's not in the office at this time," the secretary said. Francis wasn't sure whether the pain in his stomach was from disappointment or hunger. "But," she added after a pause, "we can give you an interview next Monday at two o'clock."

"Thank you," Francis said politely with a sigh of relief. "*Asante Sana*, I will be there."

"We can't promise you anything," she said, "but Mr. Maina is interviewing people for future openings." His spirits fell again; it didn't sound promising.

"I'll be there Monday at two." Francis said and hung up.

"Get the job?" Mr. Njoroge asked.

Francis tried to smile. "Only an interview."

Mr. Njoroge sat in a chair opposite Francis and crossed his legs. He looked as if he might be settling down for a chat which made Francis uncomfortable. He didn't know how to talk to important men. Now that his phone call was made, he wanted to get outside where he could relax.

"So your name is Francis Mataba." Mr. Njoroge said, and Francis knew he had listened to every word. "Where is your home district?"

"I come from Molo," Francis said. His body grew tense, his leg muscles ached.

"Your family lives there, of course?"

"Only my mother. She still farms a *shamba* a few kilometers outside Molo," Francis said, offering as little information as possible without seeming rude.

"Do you have a wife and children?"

Francis shook his head. "Not yet." He felt ashamed. His uncles had been pressuring him to get married and have sons, but he had no money to pay the bride's parents, and he knew his uncles could not afford to pay. He stared at the floor, his eyes tracing the pattern on the Indian carpet.

"Then you have only yourself?"

"Yes," Francis said, raising his eyes to look straight at Mr. Njoroge. He wondered why he was asking so many questions.

"What is your work experience, young man?" Mr. Njoroge continued, businesslike.

"I worked for the Fathers when I was in school."

"Where did you go to school?" He studied Francis as if examining an employee.

"St. Andrew's." Francis was proud he had attended such a good school. When he saw Mr. Njoroge's surprise, he added. "I had a scholarship."

"You must have been a good student."

"Yes," said Francis. "I was third in my class."

"Did you finish your secondary education?"

"Form IV. Here are my school papers." Francis produced a certificate from a worn and wrinkled envelope. He always carried it with him when job hunting.

Mr. Njoroge examined it and smiled. "Would you like to work for the telephone company?"

Francis stared, speechless. When he recovered his breath, he said, "I — I — I think I'd like it, but I didn't . . ."

"You didn't know we had an opening, right?"

"That's right," Francis said, still unbelieving.

Mr. Njoroge continued. "We had to let our messenger go

yesterday. He was never on time, and he wasn't reliable. I believe you will be different, right?"

Francis nodded, remembering what he had said in anger outside on the street.

"The starting salary is eight hundred shilling per month. You will be a temporary employee for the first three months. If you work out for us, your salary will be increased according to your value to the company."

Francis still couldn't think of anything to say. Everything had happened too suddenly; he couldn't believe he was going to be a working man. He could buy food, new shoes, and. . ."

"Here is an application for you to fill out and bring in with you when you come in at nine o'clock tomorrow. My assistant will train you and explain your duties."

Francis shook hands and almost forgot to say, "Thank you."

Outside, the sun seemed brighter than it had for months. He couldn't believe his good luck. He walked up the street smiling, a spring in his step. He called "*Habari ya asubuhi*" to the shoe shine man. He said "*Jambo*," to each sidewalk salesman and shook hands with some of them. He looked for the Maasai, but they were gone. He felt in his pocket for the two remaining shillings, rubbing them together with his thumb and forefinger. He thought of them as his lucky coins, wanted to keep them, and hoped he would get as much value from them as he had from the other two.

A teenage boy plays his bamboo flute outside his grandmother's hut. Boys learned to weave mats, make toys and musical instruments, and string traps for catching birds. Girls learned to cook and make clay pots for carrying and cooking. They also ran errands and helped in the fields.

Every day at sundown, children raced about the village playing with homemade toys the headman made from tree trunks and bamboo. Note the mud verandas where people rested after a hard day in the fields.

This set of simple tools was used by Headman Katuwa to carry out work necessary for farming and hunting. The hoe, scythe, and ax were used for clearing land and cultivation, the spear and club were used for hunting, and the knives were useful in cleaning game and stripping bamboo for weaving baskets.

A young mother's back serves as a table to keep the baby clean while her grandmother helps bathe her baby in cold water at the well. Grandparents, often too old to do heavy farm work, may be more active than parents in the training and care of children.

Morning and evening, women went to the well to draw water for drinking, cooking, and cleaning. the government sunk deep wells to provide clean water and improve health conditions for village people. Young woman on the right carried water in a large gourd.

The village woman's day is filled with hard work necessary for survival. Here women pound maize in mortars carved from tree trunks to remove the husk for making cornmeal mush similar to grits. The cracked grain is soaked in the river until it begins to ferment, dried in sun on sleeping mats, and then carried on her head to a grinding mill and ground into meal.

Brewing maize beer and making clay pottery were ways women earned cash income. The brewing process involved several days. After mixing ingredients in barrels, the mixture was stored in large clay pots for fermentation. News was sent to neighboring villages when the beer was ready; beer was sold by the cup. The money was often used for clothes and for children's school fees.

This child's mother had gone to the city to work while he lived with his grandmother. His grandmother was sick and could not carry him or give him proper nutrition. Babies are usually carried on their mother's backs and nursed until about age two.

Mama Nyina's Story

Mama Nyina wa Karanja sat beside the hole she was digging beneath the hedge in the corner of her *shamba*. She scratched at the dirt with her fingers, lifted the plastic bag she had buried more than a year before, and gasped. She cupped the bag in her hands and watched ants hustle among tattered remains of the one-hundred shilling notes inside. Her body convulsed as she tried not to cry out; the sound would attract attention to her hiding place, the place she called her special bank.

She had always thought of big banks in town as places for rich people to keep money — people who knew how to read and write. She had tried to deposit money in a Post Office account, but a thief had taken it, and now the thieving ants had discovered her hiding place. Tears fell, watering the large red carnations on the loose-fitting dress she wore over her shapeless body. She leaned her head against her hands; dark soil from her fingers smudged the white head cloth which had slipped over her wrinkled forehead shading her eyes. "What can I do now?" she sobbed.

Mama Nyina lived alone in a tiny mud-walled hut with a tin roof which her husband had built for her before his death many years ago. The hut, in need of repair, stood on the edge of an acre of land beside a grove of eucalyptus trees overlooking Egerton University near Njoro, Kenya. Each morning when the sun rose beyond the branches spreading delicate light over her *shamba*, a soft light saturated tree tops and roofs of large brick buildings at the University, lending to them an air of importance.

The University had always been a mysterious place to Mama Nyina. Educated men and women who taught there wore clothes like *mzungus* and seemed strangers from another world. She sometimes stopped and stared when she saw them on the road to Njoro, but they didn't see her trudging along with the leather thong strapped across her head supporting the load on her back. To them, she was just another old Kikuyu woman, and the sight of her was as common and as natural as the landscape. The people in huts around her were temporary workers at the University who came and went with dry seasons and long rains. They were strangers from many different places and tribes.

Then a professor at the University built a stone house on a plot of land beside her *shamba*. He built a fence to keep out thieves, and he planted a tall hedge to shield him from her shabby hut. The professor's daughter, who had not yet reached maturity, sometimes called to Mama Nyina as she played beside the hedge, but Mama Nyina had no relatives near. There was nobody she could trust, nobody she could go to for help. She sat on the ground with years of shredded savings in her lap, held her head in her hands, and wept.

She didn't know how much time had passed when she heard a rustle beside her and looked up into the solemn face of the professor's daughter. The girl's eyes were wide with curiosity. Her blue cotton dress, ruffled at the hem, was freshly pressed. Her hair was neat and braided close to her head. "Are you sick, Mama?" she asked.

"I am sick in my heart, child," Mama Nyina said but offered no explanation.

"Maybe I can help."

"Look, *mwana*," Mama Nyina said holding up the plastic

bag in her cupped hands like an offering. "I was saving these shillings to buy a cow that I might have milk. A man offered to sell me a heifer, but now he will sell it to somebody who has shillings."

"Where would you keep a cow? There's no place for a cow to graze?" The girl's eyes, surveying the *shamba*, rested on neat rows of vegetables and maize.

"I would build a pen," Mama Nyina said. "And I would carry gunny sacks of grass from there." She pointed toward the University. "When workers cut grass, I can collect clippings."

The girl squatted in front of Mama Nyina and stared into her wrinkled face noting that her eyes were clouded with crying and old age. The woman's mouth drooped; vertical wrinkles led into her mouth like exclamation marks.

"I'm so sorry." The girl said. "Please don't cry anymore."

"You don't understand," Mama Nyina said, "These pieces of chewed paper are my life's savings. For years, I planted beans, maize, tomatoes, carrots and cabbage. For years, I carried vegetables to market on my back all the way to Njoro. For years, I saved shillings, keeping just enough for my daily needs. And this is what happens to an honest woman." She held the plastic bag of shilling notes out toward the girl as if expecting her to perform a miracle.

The girl looked at the bag, turning her head to one side. "Maybe we can put them back together."

"No, *mwana*," Mama Nyina shook her head. "There is nothing to be done."

"My father will help you. He knows how to do everything!"

"No, child. Long ago I learned to live one day at a time, and I can still do it, even without my savings. After my husband died, I had only myself, and I remembered the wise saying of the Kikuyu elders, *bata ndurutanagwo* (One's needs are not met by other people.) I worked hard, but now I'm old. My bones ache from the cold at night. I'm tired, and I don't remember things sometimes."

"I forget things sometimes, too," she girl said. "Last week I forgot my geography book and went to school without it."

"The other day a man wanted to know how old I am, and I didn't know. I've always been told it's wrong to count cattle, or children, or the passing of years, but I would like to know how old I am." She paused, squinting at the girl's face. "Do you know how old you are, child?"

"The girl smiled. "I'm almost ten."

"I can remember things people say happened more than seventy years ago," Mama Nyina said. "Like wars and cattle raids."

The girl caught her breath. "Seventy years is a long time! How can anybody live so long?"

"Since I can't read or keep records," Mama Nyina said, "I have to believe what people tell me. I'll never know how old I am. I'm ready to die now."

The girl, still squatting, straightened her legs on the ground and sat facing the old woman. She touched Mama Nyina's calloused hands. "You don't look so old to me," she said with a tremor in her voice. "I think you are — well, — uh — I think you're beautiful!"

"I'm ready to die now," Mama Nyina repeated, fingering the bag of shredded shillings. "I've lived long enough."

The girl stood up, studying the old woman with troubled eyes. She shifted her weight from one foot to the other and wiped her sweating palms on the skirt of her clean dress. Nobody had ever told her such dark secrets.

Mama Nyina stared at the ground, her shoulders hunched, her head bent, her wrinkled hands still grasping the plastic bag.

"You don't understand, *mwana*. You cannot know what it's like to be old and without children."

The girl turned, bolted like a frightened antelope, her voice trailing behind her as she ran. "Don't go away, Mama. I will find help."

"No," Mama Nyina called, "there is no help. Come back, child. Come back! Tell me your name." But the girl had disappeared beyond the hedge.

Alone again, Mama Nyina felt empty inside. She gathered up the bag of torn shilling notes and went to her hut. Inside, the house was dark, uninviting; there were no windows. The low doorway spread a trapezoid of yellow sunlight on the earth floor. She dropped the bag on a small table covered with a faded crocheted spread she had made when her hands were not crippled with arthritis. Her thin body moved as if she carried a great weight. She lay on her bed mat in a stupor of fatigue, her eyes closed.

She didn't know how long she had been resting when she heard a man's voice calling at her door. "*Natia. Wequo*. Are you in?"

"*Ye ndequo*. Yes I am in." Struggling to her feet, she recognized the man standing in her doorway as the professor who lived in the stone house next door. He was a thin man with a broad face. His hair was clipped short above gold-rimmed glasses, and he looked impressive in a dark business suit. She had seen him go and come in his red Peugeot, but he had always looked past her, through her, and into the space beyond. She didn't think he knew she existed. He was an important man, an educated man; she couldn't find words to speak. When she saw the girl standing behind him, she was more at ease.

"*Natie*, Mama," the professor said, respecting her age. "I'm your neighbor, Mr. Mwangi, and this is my daughter Muthoni."

His voice was quiet; he was a man to be trusted.

Mama Nyina's only chair, a chair with a broken back, sat outside under a eucalyptus tree; she stepped through the doorway and invited him to sit. She was glad she had swept the bare yard earlier that morning; she wanted him to think well of her. She stood before him wondering what to do, then she sat on the ground facing him. She looked at Muthoni's clean blue dress with the white ruffle around the hem and decided not to invite her to sit on the ground. She waited for the professor to speak.

"My daughter, Muthoni, tells me you need help."

"There is no help. I have lost everything."

Professor Mwangi looked serious. Those were words he expected to hear from an old woman needing assistance. "Do you have children who can help you?"

"I had eight children, but my only living child is a girl. She has been married more than twenty years and lives with her husband in Nairobi."

"Do you see her often?"

Mama Nyina shook her head. "She belongs to her husband's clan. She comes to see me once a year when her husband gives permission. For that I'm grateful."

"It is too bad you have no sons."

"They died when they were children. Some died of smallpox in the epidemic. Others died of diarrhea or a pain in the chest."

"And your husband?"

"He passed away many years ago. I don't remember how many. He died of malaria."

Professor Mwangi looked about him at the little hut which needed repair and at the garden with vegetables in neat rows, and then his eyes fastened on the wrinkled face of the woman. "Do you live here alone? Have you no relatives?"

"Aiee. I'm strong," Mama Nyina said, flexing her right arm. "I can carry water from the river. I can carry firewood from the lumber mill. I can hoe in the shamba. I can still carry vegetables to the market to earn money, but I can't find a safe place to keep shillings."

"Why don't you put your money in a bank?"

Mama Nyina looked at him, wondering if he had ever lived in a village and if he knew how country people thought about banks. "Banks are for rich people who know how to read and write," she said. "The men in the cages are thieves. I hid my money in a secret place in my *shamba*, but the ants are also thieves."

Muthoni stood behind her father's chair pulling at a sprig of hair behind her right ear. Professor Mwangi looked at Mama Nyina for a long time and said nothing. He studied the deep wrinkles, the soiled head cloth covering her short grey hair, and the faded brown dress from which red carnations seemed to grow out of clay. He noted the indentation across her forehead, the mark of elderly Kikuyu women who had carried the burdens of the tribe on a head-strap since childhood. And he noted the slump of her shoulders, a deformity from a lifetime of transporting heavy weight. He sometimes wished Kikuyu women carried things on their heads like women from some other tribes. They would be more graceful, he thought, and they wouldn't shuffle when they walked. But his tribe believed carrying things on the head damaged the brain. He dismissed this thought by shifting his weight in the chair. He wanted to get back to work. Muthoni had disturbed him while he was grading exams. He looked again at the old woman. She was not his responsibility. He was only doing this to please Muthoni. He had his own relatives to support, nephews to send to school; he was in no position to take on more trouble.

"Let me see the damage the ants did to your savings," he said, trying to recall the garbled story Muthoni had told him in her excitement.

Mama Nyina went inside the hut and returned with the plastic bag filled with torn shillings. "Look!" she said, thrusting the bag at him with both hands, her voice quivering.

"Aiee, Mama," Professor Mwangi said, examining the bag. "I will try to advise you. It's my opinion you should put your money in a Post Office Savings Account. The Post Office will give you a small book, and each time you make a deposit, a clerk will paste stamps inside."

"Once I had a savings account at the Post Office," Mama Nyina said. "I will never put money there again."

"Why not?"

"People can't be trusted."

"What happened?" Professor Mwangi shifted his weight again, crossed his legs, and settled back to listen. Muthoni moved toward him, touching his shoulder and the back of the broken chair.

"I had enough shillings from selling vegetables at the market to open an account," she said. "I took my money there, and they gave me a pass book. I didn't go again for many months until I had saved a thousand shillings. When I reached the post office that day, I was late. A long line had already formed of people holding savings pass books in their hands." She paused.

"Yes. Go on."

"It was a long walk to Njoro, and my legs were hurting. I stood to one side wondering whether I should trail at the end of the line or go back home, but I knew it was dangerous to keep so much money in my hut. Then a postal worker at the registered letter window asked, 'May I help you, Mama?' He seemed to have no work to do, so when he offered to help me, I was grateful. I told him I wanted to bank some money and handed it to him with the savings book. He disappeared for some time and returned later, smiling."

"Please continue," Professor Mwangi said.

"The man handed my savings book to me and said, 'Goodbye, Mama. Take care of that savings book. You should not let people see it. What is inside should be top secret.' I thanked him for the service and his good advice. I went home and hid the book in a safe place in my hut. I didn't show the savings book to anybody. Months later, my daughter came from Nairobi to see me. She was worried about my welfare so I took the savings book out to show her that I was all right, and I told her about the last big deposit. She took the book in her hands — like this — and looked at it." Mama Nyina held her hands together before her face like an open book." 'Are you sure you made a deposit, Mama?' my daughter asked with a surprised look.'"

"The deposit for one thousand shillings is in the book," I said. "A man helped me so I would not have to stand in line."

Mama Nyina placed her hands on her cheeks. "My daughter put her hands to her face like this and said, 'You have been robbed, Mama. The man took your money. There is no deposit here.'"

"I tore my hair, and then I cried. I have always taken care of myself and my own affairs, but I felt helpless. I asked my daughter, 'What can I do?'"

"'That was a long time ago, mama,' my daughter said. 'We don't even know the man's name. There is no way to identify him.'"

"I regretted the day I ever opened a Post Office Savings Account, and I swore I would never save money in that place again. I decided to open my own bank account in my *shamba*. I didn't know ants would eat paper money."

Mama Nyina looked tired when she finished telling her

story. She stared at the ground. Professor Mwangi sat in silence staring into the distance, thinking. Muthoni stood behind him. The only sounds were the distant bleating of goats.

Professor Mwangi opened the plastic bag and examined the damaged shillings. He took out small pieces and squinted at them against the sunlight. "I believe I can help you," he said, still examining the shredded paper.

Mama Nyina's face brightened and then grew cautious. Educated people know how to do so many mysterious things, she thought, but can they be trusted?

"Yes," the professor said, holding a piece of ragged shillings note out for her to examine. "There are serial numbers on many of these pieces. I will go with you to the Kenya Commercial Bank to see if we can recover some of your loss."

"Do you really think we could do that?" Mama Nyina cried, her eyes bright. "Do you really think so?"

"Yes, Mama," the professor said, "but only from these notes that still have a serial number on them."

"Oh, thank you," Mama Nyina sighed. "I will be happy. Just tell me when to go." She smiled for the first time, showing ragged, yellow teeth.

"I will go with you on Thursday, and then we will go to the Post Office and re-open your account. Even if the ants didn't eat paper money," the professor scolded as if talking to a child, "it wouldn't be safe for you to keep money in your *shamba*. Thugs might learn you have it and beat you to make you tell where it is."

"I have been twice beaten," Mama Nyina said, hesitating to take his advice. "When an old woman can't read or write, she has to believe what people tell her, and they sometimes tell her bad things."

"Take somebody you can trust with you when you deposit

money. Since you have no relatives near, my wife or I will try to find time to go with you."

Tears clouded Mama Nyina's eyes. "Thank you. I'm so grateful."

After the professor and Muthoni were gone, Mama Nyina sat for a long time watching the sun play with light and shadow on the eucalyptus leaves swaying in the breeze at the edge of her *shamba*. She felt a warm glow, an inner peace, a renewed hope for the days ahead. After so many lonely years, she was no longer alone. She saw before her the bright face of Muthoni and the kind face of the professor who knew how to do important things. But years had made her cautious. "Can I trust him?" she said aloud. "He seems all right, but can I be be sure?"

She rose, unsteady on her feet, shuffled into her hut and prepared to do those things she knew how to do to remain self-sufficient. She placed the leather strap of the water jug across her forehead and adjusted the keg on her back. "One's needs are not met by other people," she mumbled as she trudged to Njoro River to get water, "but sometimes one is forced to take chances."

Last Sabbatical

Professor Lang looked at his watch. "Let's go back to our hotel now. It's late. We've seen enough hotels for one day."

"Just one more, Raymond. Please?" Maggie begged. "I want to have a definite suggestion for the children when I write."

He didn't want to tell Maggie how confused he was by the noise of Nairobi's traffic jams, honking horns, squealing brakes, and reckless drivers playing bluff at intersections. He didn't want to tell her how uneasy he felt amidst the sea of humanity surging forward at bus stops, and the hawkers who packed every corner of their little trucks and vans with people, sometimes loading them on top or letting them hang out back doors with clothes flapping in wind.

Since her stroke, although it was a slight one, she had become almost childlike. He found himself humoring her about small things and wanting to protect her. In Nairobi, he felt the need to protect her from the stories he'd heard about strong young men walking faceless among crowds, snatching purses or jewelry, or attacking tourists in groups. He knew at their age they were especially vulnerable. He walked faster.

"We don't have to make a decision right away." He squeezed her arm and pulled her along past flowering bougainvillaea between Central and Uhuru Parks near the end of the rush hour. His head was capped with a bush of white hair and his eyes rimmed with gold-framed bifocals, but his back was straight and his build large and athletic. He wore his dark suit with dignity.

Maggie, his petite wife, trotted now and then to keep pace with his rapid stride, making the limp in her left leg more pronounced. Her greying hair framed a sweet face. Age lines at the corners of her mouth and pale blue eyes were as prominent as tribal scars. She clung to his arm. An African basket she had bought that morning from a street vendor swung from one shoulder.

When he said nothing more, Maggie said, "This will be their last sabbatical with us, and I want it to be special."

Professor Lang knew she was right. He was past seventy, and when he went back home to Illinois, he planned to retire. Although there was no retirement age for professors, he was tired of dealing with ambitious young men competing for tenure and jockeying for important positions. The fact of his mortality struck him last year when an awful tiredness came over him and he went home from the office early at least twice a week to nap before dinner.

"The kids are coming to visit with us," he said. "Our children aren't fussy about where they sleep. They never were."

"But I want everything to be just right. I'd like to match hotel reservations with their personalities."

Dr. Lang chuckled and patted her arm. "Trust you to think of something like that, Maggie. That's one of the things I've always liked about you. You're so creative." Maggie smiled. "But you've taken on an impossible task. Their personalities are all so different."

"Ray Junior is a history buff," she said. "I'm sure he's reading books about Kenyan tribes and the British Colonial Period. I've thought about a hotel with lovely old gardens and a British flavor."

"And what about his wife Anna?"

"Oh, you know Anna. She's so good-natured she'll go along with anything Ray wants to do."

"She's like you," Raymond said.

"And George's wife, Millicent, likes to shop," Maggie said. "She likes being at the center of things. I'd match her with a downtown hotel. Maybe the Hilton would be best for all of them. They could always go to dinner at the old hotels and look at the gardens.

"What about George? You know how independent he is," Raymond said.

"If Millicent's happy, he's happy. From what I can see, he goes his own way and lets her do what she likes."

"You have one big fault, Maggie," Raymond said. "You've always made decisions for the children and you're still doing it." He wanted to say, "It's time you let go of the children and start thinking about me," but he didn't want to sound selfish. She had been a good mother.

"Nonsense! I haven't made decisions for them in years!"

"Then stop being a mother hen. Let them do this on their own."

"They are on their own. They're financially independent and haven't asked us for a thing." They walked in silence.

Recently, instead of thinking about the future, he had thought more and more about the past, other sabbaticals, when he took his young family to India, and then took his teenagers to Peru to study Spanish and the Indian cultures. He and Maggie had gone to Australia alone while both boys were at universities, but he had sent them plane tickets for Christmas vacation.

"You know, Maggie," he said, still thinking about Australia. "I think we are going to have the best year of our lives here."

"Oh, yes," she agreed. "I love the scenery, the huge craters in the Rift Valley, the Maasai herding cattle in those red plaid blankets." She squeezed his arm, remembering their weekend trip to Amboceli Game Park and their visit to a nearby Maasai Village.

"I like the rich farms in the uplands," Raymond added, "and the lakes pink with flamingoes. And my colleagues at Egerton University who are friendly and congenial."

"Give me a shilling, mother," a voice pleaded. A barefoot child wearing dirt-caked shorts and an oversized fedora trotted beside her, his grimy hand outstretched. Maggie started. She hadn't heard the boy approach. "Please, Mother. I'm hungry. Give me a shilling."

Maggie dug into the basket for her coin purse as she walked. The boy's eyes followed the movements of her hand. A saccharin voice added, "Ten shillings? Please, mother? For food?"

"Don't do that, Maggie," Raymond scolded. "How many times have people told you not to take money out on the street?" He reached into his pocket, drew out a handful of coins, and dropped them into the boy's cupped hands without looking at them.

"Now, go away," he said, but the boy followed at a short distance.

"I have most of our money in my money belt," Maggie whispered. "I don't have much in my coin purse."

"It doesn't matter. You have to be careful."

Maggie and Raymond reached the Kenyatta Avenue roundabout. Their pace increased as they hurried toward their hotel and Maggie found it harder to keep up. The air grew chilly; Maggie shivered. Evening rush-hour traffic thinned. The park looked deserted except for a few men strolling along paths beside flowering shrubs—poinsettias in full bloom, oleander, delicate rust and red bougainvillaea clinging like tissue paper to prickly hedge.

Without warning, a click of rapid footsteps, a surprise slap on Maggie's arm, a lightning tug at her wrist, and a flash of black. Her basket was gone. Two men raced across the park, one of them swinging her basket like a pendulum.

"Thief! Thief!" Maggie shrieked.

"Be quiet, Maggie!"

Maggie had read in a safari magazine that if someone tries to steal your purse, you should yell, 'Thief' and the good *wananchi* will come to help. She congratulated herself mentally that she still had presence of mind to remember what to do. She was always forgetting things since she'd had her stroke.

Raymond watched the men disappear behind shrubbery.

"Do something, Raymond!"

"There's nothing we can do, Maggie. Let them go."

"Can we help?" Three young Africans surrounded them. The men were clean, and well-groomed, neatly dressed in sport shirts and polyester trousers. They looked respectable.

"Are you hurt?" one asked, smiling. He had a kind face and a wide gap between two large front teeth.

"No," Maggie said, "but you can help us. Those men took my basket with my coin purse inside."

"Oh, how shameful," another said, clicking his tongue. "They're bad people." His speech was a mixture of British and tribal accents.

"Did you lose your money?" the third man inquired. He was small and lean and looked older than the others.

"No," Maggie said, "but I'd like to have my basket back. It had important papers in it."

"We can help you," the older man said. "Come with us."

The three men started across the park motioning for Maggie and Raymond to follow.

"Come back, Maggie," Raymond called when he saw Maggie running behind them. "Come back! There's nothing we can do!"

"They said they'd help us," Maggie called over her shoulder.

Raymond followed, chagrined at Maggie's childlike trust in strangers. He ran after her to bring her back.

The men wheeled, and with the agility of big cats at Amboceli, pounced, grabbed Raymond by the shoulders, twisted his arms behind him, pushed him to the ground. Maggie screamed. The man with the kind face locked his arm around Maggie's neck. Her head felt full, her vision blurred, then darkness. The kind man let her fall with a thud and turned to Raymond.

While two men held Dr. Lang on the ground, the other pulled and tore at his back pockets taking his billfold, coins, keys, receipts. They turned him over, stripped off his suit coat. Raymond kicked, pounded with fists, jabbed with elbows, but he was one against three. They pounded his face, ripped off his belt, and tore the front pockets from his trousers. They snatched his shoes and socks and ran. It was over in seconds.

Blackness spread before Raymond's eyes, then cleared. Through twilight, he saw the top of Maggie's head where she lay in an awkward sprawl. He crawled to her, flinching at pain in his wrenched shoulders.

"Wake up, Maggie. Wake up!" he cried, his voice hoarse. He shook her, but she lay limp on the ground. "My God! They've killed her," he moaned."Oh, my God!" His shoulders shook. He looked about for help, smothered by the rapid beating of his heart.

Raymond saw Maggie's eyelids flutter. She looked up at white clouds in a twilight sky, and then at Raymond's face bending over her's. She groaned.

"Maggie, are you all right?" he whispered, wanting to ask, "Are you alive?" but not wanting to say the words.

"Oh, Raymond. What did they do to you? Where are your glasses?"

"Can you get up, Maggie?"

"I think I'm all right," she said, sitting up. "I must have fainted."

"Then let's get the hell out of here!" He helped her to her feet and walked with his arm around her toward the sidewalk through flowering fushia, marigolds, geraniums.

"Something's happened to my neck," Maggie said, rubbing the vertebrae at the back of her head. "Are you hurt, Raymond?"

"Nothing's broken, but I'll be sore."

"What happened to your glasses?"

"I don't know."

"And you have no shoes!"

"They took them. Our passports, credit cards, everything".

"Oh Raymond," Maggie wailed, "but I still have my money belt. At least we're not penniless."

Raymond was also limping when they came in sight of their hotel where the uniformed night watchman stood large and composed by the doorway, a heavy club swinging from his wide leather belt.

"I dread going in," Maggie said. "We look awful." Raymond helped Maggie as she stumbled up the steps.

"Don't worry about the way we look," Raymond said, patting her arm. "People will understand. We need help, and we have to notify the police."

The hotel lobby was bustling with activity. A safari bus had arrived with a tour group from Germany. Men in casual dress or safari suits, middle-aged women in baggy slacks and flowing skirts, young people in tight jeans or shorts stood in groups waiting for room assignments around clusters of luggage. Their tour leader, a tall Englishman, argued with the desk clerk; there had been a mistake in the number of rooms reserved for his group. An African from Senegal was trying to register, but the desk clerk couldn't understand his French. A man who looked Lebanese yelled for his room key. People relaxing in soft lounge chairs looked at Maggie and Raymond and then past them into the street.

At the counter, Raymond squeezed between the Lebanese and the man from Senegal trying to attract a desk clerk's attention. "Please sir . . ."

"Just a moment," the clerk said without looking up.

"I'd like to . . ."

"You'll have to wait your turn, sir."

"But my wife and I . . ."

"We'll be with you in a moment." The clerk's voice was harsh. "We're very busy."

"I need to call the police!" Raymond insisted, raising his voice.

The clerk paused and stiffened, holding the cap of his ballpoint pen against the lapel of his dark suit. "Do you have a problem?"

"My wife and I have been robbed and assaulted."

"On hotel property?" he asked, his eyes wide.

"No. In the park."

"Only security can help you." He regarded Raymond through lidded eyes, his lips tight. He disappeared through an open door to the left and returned immediately. "Our security man has just stepped out. What's your room number?"

"I need to make a police report," Raymond insisted. "Can't you call the police?"

"This is a job for security. Tell me your room number."

"Room number 428."

"The police can't do a thing," a clipped British accent said in his ear. Raymond turned to see a thin weathered woman with graying blond hair and a bitter face where the Lebanese had been. "I've lived here thirty years," she said. "I know for a fact the police can't do a thing to help you."

The clerk handed Raymond his key, eyeing his tousled hair and bruised face with mild distaste. "Wait in your room," he said. "I'll send our security man up as soon as he returns."

Inside 428, Raymond looked about him. The room was ordinary for the price he had paid. In fact, it was shabby, and he'd received shabby treatment. Depression settled like a weight. He'd been shamelessly violated, and his feeling of impotence frightened him. He wanted to strike out, but there was not a thing or a person related to the incident he could slam his fist into. If he could only turn back time. If he and Maggie had only done something different. Maggie, sitting on the edge of her bed, began to cry. He thought he knew how she felt. The shock was wearing off.

"We could have been killed!" Maggie's voice choked with indignation.

"But we weren't killed. Try to think of it that way." He wanted to reassure her, but his knees trembled and his wrenched shoulders ached.

She turned her face to his. "Do you realize, Raymond, that we've traveled in almost every country in the world, and we've never had anything like this happen?"

"We've been lucky." His voice was quiet with a calmness he didn't feel. "This could have happened anywhere, even at home."

He looked at Maggie sitting hunched on the soiled bedspread rubbing her neck. He had always protected her, and now he couldn't throw off guilt for allowing her to be in a position of risk. She looked exhausted. He hadn't noticed before how old she was. The creases around her eyes and at the corners of her mouth were deeper than he remembered. The years had rushed past, one pummeling over the other headlong into old age. The two of them had done interesting things together, and there was no denying how close they had been. What he felt for her now was not passion and not exactly love; it was a great need, a need for loyalty in an uncaring world, a need to know that he came first.

"Do you want to go home, Maggie?" It was not a question he meant to ask, but now that he'd asked it, he held his breath, afraid of what she might say. He hoped she would say they were in this together, only the two of them mattered, and everything was going to be all right. But Maggie studied the brown tweed carpet before raising her eyes to his bruised and swollen face.

"No," she said. "But promise me you won't tell the children."

Misfits

Pat Thatcher was boiling the day's supply of drinking water. She glanced out the kitchen window and saw Sama returning from his daily errands empty handed. Long ago she had stopped going to the fly-infested market with its suffocating odors of dried and decaying fish where she had to bargain for everything. Sama could bargain better and he liked to do it. She had also told him to see Tote-Man, her taxi driver and ask him to take her to Bo. Sama opened the screen door and let it slam behind him.

"Tote-Man's wife says he can't come." His face wore an expression of delight, a look she had seen on faces of people who liked to tease Tote-Man.

"Is he sick?"

"He's in jail."

"Why?" Pat asked, slamming a lid on the pot of boiling water.

"Stealing."

"That must be a mistake," she said. She had not known Tote-Man to be dishonest. Unlike other drivers, he had never overcharged her.

"No," Sama said, shaking his head. "His wife told me."

"Where is he?" Pat asked.

"He's there." Sama pointed with his forefinger in the direction of the village police station.

She sent Sama back to the market to get the vegetables she

would have to soak in chlorine water before her husband, an A.I.D. worker, came home from the rice fields. At the moment, she wished for the luxury of a telephone, a convenience she took for granted back home in Iowa. Brushing the thought aside, she washed perspiration from her face, drew a clean sleeveless house dress over her head, and slipped her feet into comfortable sandals. Hesitating at the door, she returned to the bedroom for a wide-brimmed straw hat and perched it on top of her head without looking in the mirror. She dreaded the dusty two-mile walk to the station in broiling sun.

She was not accustomed to walking, an activity incompatible with her obesity, and disliked it intensely. Walking provided little mental stimulation, allowing her to dwell on her unpleasant situation which the State Department pamphlets called "culture shock," but which she called "hardship" pure and simple. Today she tried to forget her personal discomfort by concentrating on Tote-Man. By birth he was Lebanese. He was married to an African woman, and he lived like an African in a mud and thatched hut. He spoke English and Krio, a mixture of Portuguese, English, and African dialects, as fluently as his native language.

Tote-Man was not rich like many Lebanese who came to Sierra Leone to make a fortune in business or serve as advisers to government officials. He drove a taxi and was known as a competent mechanic who could keep his small fleet of rickety Peugeots running long after unavailable engine parts deteriorated and fenders rusted out. He was also less reckless than other drivers on the potholed roads. People felt safer riding with him.

Everyone in the village knew Tote-Man when his name was mentioned. They said he was "crazy," touched fingertips to their foreheads, smirked, and shook their heads as if holding back some delicious secret. They seemed to enjoy telling how he had suffered a nervous breakdown although nobody seemed to remember the exact details. The story had been told so often everybody believed it and accepted it as a fact, but Pat wasn't convinced. She had seen little beyond his good-natured clowning.

"Why do people say Tote-Man is crazy?" Pat asked a driver one day who was laughing about how another driver had poured water in Tote-Man's gas tank. He acted out the incident and interrupted his narrative with derisive laughter.

"He does funny things," the driver said. "He makes silly faces when he talks, and he pretends to be dancing when he repairs his motor." He tossed the butt of his hand-rolled cigarette into the hedge and shrugged. "And he does not follow our customs." Pat had said nothing at the time, but she remembered her anger at Tote-Man's shabby treatment.

She was so tired when she walked through the center of town, she hardly noticed the familiar scenes on either side of her—the government hospital with its Indian doctors, the cinder block church with the steeple bell which didn't ring, and rows of square mud houses where tailors sat by doors pedaling ancient, hand-powered sewing machines. The stench of rot and decay was all around her. She hoped in time she would get used to it.

The houses at the far edge of town had more yard space where mango, lime, and breadfruit trees spread over bare, packed soil. An occasional banana plant grew beside houses, and now and then papaya stood like sentinels topped with clusters of ripening fruit. She walked past scatters of anthills shaped like mushrooms. The trees and shrubs she found so interesting at first held no fascination for her now. At last, she saw the rusting tin roof of the police station in the distance and tried to return to the reason for her errand. She wanted to plan what she would do and say once she reached the station, but her thoughts drifted to the first time she saw Tote-Man.

Pat had been in the country less than a month when she traveled by government bus to Bo early one morning to search for a wandering merchant who had gained a reputation for peddling his wife's gara, exquisite tie-dyed fabric tinted with the natural dyes of indigo and cola nut. By late afternoon, she was waiting with the unwrapped cloth in her arms under the tall fig tree at the edge of town where taxis load and unload.

Pat looked around her at the sea of black faces and felt panic. She did not yet know how to deal with vendors who closed in upon her, encircled her, and pressured her to buy things she didn't want. She was always torn by a painful ambivalence—a mixture of annoyance and fear at their persistent begging and tugging at her arm, and guilt that she couldn't give money to everyone in need. Sometimes she bought from the ragged, emaciated children who, she was told, were beaten when they went home at night if they didn't bring money to relatives giving them shelter. Sometimes when she refused, the children begged pitifully for coins or asked her, a stranger, to pay their school fees. They always had a sad story of death, hunger, or disease which they insisted on telling even when her pain caused her to turn away.

Standing in shade of the tree, she watched vendors hawk spicy food on rusted wire grills. Children clustered about her begging her to buy fruit and fried pastries from soiled boxes and frayed baskets, but today they drifted away when she smiled and shook her head. Lean, hungry dogs prowled through the crowd sniffing for crumbs and goats wandered on the fringes foraging for dry wisps of grass.

"*Padi a want di lohri*!" a woman screeched, impatient for a taxi.

Other women in long flowered dresses, clutching hands of

fretting children, argued in Krio about who would ride next. As taxis arrived, crowds rushed at drivers, pushing and shoving to get the doors open and pack themselves inside. The people waiting far outnumbered the taxis which would be available before nightfall; she feared she would be stranded.

A grey Peugeot, mottled with rust, skidded to a stop in front of her. As the crowd swept her forward, the driver, a tall, thin man with a shock of straight brown hair, got out of his taxi and motioned her to the driver's side of the car, the choice seat beside him. She guessed from his loose-jointed build, swarthy crooked face, and huge feet too big for his runover shoes that this was Tote-Man all the taxi drivers talked about and ridiculed. She liked him immediately.

Amid pushing and shoving, Tote-Man drove off yelling, "No more! No more!" His tires grated on gravel, leaving a whirlwind of dust. Like an afterthought, the back doors were closed by passengers. Four people sat in front and seven in back, wedged in every available space, and on laps, arms twined self-consciously, bracing for balance.

Pat hugged the gara to her and tried to imagine herself small. She was nauseated by the stench of stale sweat. The passenger beside her was holding his wife on his lap and the woman's high heels dug painfully into Pat's right ankle. Intent on enduring close quarters, nobody spoke for several miles. An African man wearing a dirty cowboy shirt said something to Tote-Man in Krio. He spoke so rapidly Pat caught only a fragment, "*yu na krabit man*," and knew he was teasing Tote-Man about being stingy. Tote-Man responded with clowning and good humor. The comedy of the remaining conversation had no meaning for Pat, but women in the back seat giggled. As the verbal exchanges continued, Pat listened to Tote-Man's quick, staccato responses in Krio and watched his loose-jointed arms jerk comically as he maneuvered the taxi. She believed Tote-Man was playing the fool for their entertainment.

The teasing was interrupted when the taxi stopped for a road blockade. A policeman in full uniform stood beside the road waving his club. Tote-Man parked and waited.

"Come with me," the policeman said, leading Tote-Man to a crude thatched shelter a short distance away.

Soon after her arrival, Pat had been stopped by a policeman who squinted dramatically at her passport and pretended to find some irregularity. He had confiscated it while he consulted another policeman. She was frightened at the time, not knowing that was a method of extracting bribes. He eventually returned her passport to her. After that she pretended innocence with the same results. She was afraid the policeman might demand her passport now and the taxi would be detained or she would be stranded on the road.

Pat strained to hear the conversations of the two men speaking in English. The policeman flailed his arms and scolded Tote-Man, who stood with his hands in the pockets of his worn trousers listening patiently. Finally, he scraped both feet backward like a rooster scratching for grain. When the policeman raised his voice, Pat heard the words distinctly.

"If you ever do that again, you will not drive a taxi on this road."

Tote-Man handed the policeman money and walked back to the car. As he drove away, Pat waited for an explanation, but none came.

"Why did he say that to you?" Pat asked when she could bear the suspense no longer.

"I refused to stop last time. I ran through the blockade."

"Do you always have to pay?"

"Yes, but I've already paid thirty leones today, and I can't afford to pay more. I won't make any money today."

"Does the government know?" Pat asked.

Tote-Man laughed. He dusted the fingers of his right hand over the left palm and explained that government money to pay policemen often disappeared. Nobody was sure what happened to it. Needing to support their families, policemen set up road blocks to collect money from travelers. Since there were few private cars, taxis bore most of the burden.

"The policemen say we overload our taxis," Tote-Man continued, "and that's illegal. We pay them and they don't report us."

"Then why do you overload your taxis if it's illegal?" Pat asked.

"Tote-Man laughed again. "We'd have to pay anyway. We have to overload to make any money."

From that day, Pat took a special liking to Tote-Man and sent for him when she needed a taxi. Without intending to, she took on the role of patron, a role expected of Americans who, the villagers believed, found money growing on trees as plentiful as leaves in groves of mango. She knew she wanted to help Tote-Man because he was dependable and tried to be honest in a system impossible to break. On long trips he sometimes told her about his family. His first wife had died of childbirth fever, and his son, whose body was riddled with nodules of larvae, would eventually die of river blindness; treatment was too expensive for him to afford. She sometimes gave him tips amounting to more than he could earn in a long day of driving.

"That's too much, Madam," he said each time. When she insisted he take the money for treatment for his son, he accepted. She wanted to be generous because he had not overcharged her like the others drivers.

Pat's cotton dress, soaked with perspiration, was clinging to her large shapeless body by the time she arrived at the concrete-block police station. She tugged at her skirt self-consciously. She removed the straw hat and ran her fingers through the damp hair pasted close to her forehead. The guard stared at her.

"I came to see Tote-Man," she said.

"That will be thirty *leones*," he said. His voice was crisp and businesslike, but his manner was friendly. His price was more than she expected; he'd asked what he thought she could pay.

"I don't have thirty *leones*, and I don't have to pay you." Pat said, feeling her anger rise. "And I will see him."

The guard shifted papers on his makeshift desk and repeated. "That will be thirty *leones*."

"I will wait," Pat said.

She sat on the battered wooden bench which creaked from her weight and crossed her arms. She had played the game before, and she knew he would eventually let her in when he was convinced she didn't intend to pay. She stared at the peeling paint on the walls and the rust on the corrugated tin roof, but she also watched the guard as he moved about pretending to ignore her. She looked at her watch; almost an hour had passed when he said, "You can go in now."

He led her down a hallway to a room with bars on the windows. The room was bare except for a sleeping mat, a chamber pot, a tin pitcher of water and a cup placed precariously on the edge of a crude wooden table. She saw no evidence he had been fed. He seemed surprised to see her, but he smiled that crooked smile which always made his pinched face look younger.

"Why didn't you tell me you needed money?" she asked. "They told me you are in here for stealing."

He smiled, showing large front teeth, and shook his head. "Who told you that?"

"Sama."

"I don't know why I'm here," he said. "They haven't told me. The guard hinted I may have connections with the C.I.A.

"Do you?" Pat asked. "Do they have proof?"

"They don't need proof," he said. "The guard said that because I drive for you, I might have connections with the C.I.A"

He paused. His face wore the expression of a child who doesn't know why he's being punished. "What is the C.I.A?"

Pat couldn't believe he didn't know, but she tried to explain. She decided not to tell him officials in some countries use the C.I.A as an excuse to hold people illegally for other reasons.

"What can I do to help you?" Pat asked.

He shook his head. He didn't know.

"I will go to the officials," Pat offered.

He shook his head again. "I'm not rich. I have no power."

"Why do you think you're here?" Pat asked.

"I don't cooperate with them," he said, nodding toward the door. "Sometimes I refuse to pay at the blockade when they want too much money."

"I will go to government officials," Pat said again. "I will explain."

He looked at her steadily. He smiled suddenly, but there was a shadow of pain in his eyes which lingered in Pat's memory.

"I have enemies," he said. "Some drivers are jealous. They think I make a lot of money. The policemen want more money. There is nothing you can do."

Pat wasn't sure whether there was nothing she could do or whether there was nothing he wanted her to do.

"I should have listened to my wife," he said as Pat turned to leave. "She told me to get medicine from the African doctor to rub on my face, my hands, my chest," He demonstrated, pretending to rub the medicine on his body as he spoke. "She said I was careless. They would be afraid to do this to me if I had used medicine."

Pat felt a kinship with this homely man with the crooked face caught between two cultures. "He's like me," she thought. "He doesn't fit." Was her friendship responsible in some way for his arrest? She turned to look at him again as she left. He seemed so vulnerable.

"I'll come again tomorrow," she said. "We must plan."

Pat took a different route back to her house. She knew the village people were already gossiping about her visit. She recognized them as a jealous lot when two women came to her house to complain that she lived in a better house than they could own. "Why should you have these things when we can't have them?" they had asked. She also knew they watched comings and goings with morbid curiosity and envy. "News travels fast," she thought, "for a place with no telephones." As she walked, she made a mental list of the letters she would write in Tote-Man's behalf and the people she would see.

Early next morning, Pat made her way to the police station with a list of names tucked into the pocket of her cotton dress; she wanted his approval before she acted. She felt foolish meddling with an affair which didn't directly concern her, but she was convinced she could never be like the middle-aged American housewives she knew living in Sierra Leone who were afraid to venture out without husbands and who drank too much behind locked doors. She walked past a row of dying trees hung with nests of bright weaver birds. She barely heard their frantic chirping and fluttering; she was preparing for a mental test of wills.

When she entered, the guard was rummaging through folders stacked on a table in the corner of the room. She knew he saw her, but he turned his back and appeared to be examining the folders, deep in concentration.

"I came to see Tote-Man," Pat said, expecting the usual request to be paid.

He looked up, his face bright with recognition as if he had only just noticed her.

"He's not here."

"Was he released?"

"He was transferred to Freetown."

Pat tried to hide her disappointment. "On what charge?"

The guard studied her with an expression of distaste, contempt. . .perhaps contempt for all Americans. . . or contempt for women who meddle in men's affairs. "He said some bad things about our government," the guard said, "and that is forbidden."

Pat didn't believe him. She remembered Tote-Man's refusal to pay a bribe at the roadblock, his explanation of why bribes were necessary, his alleged C.I.A. connections, but she didn't remember hearing him say anything against the government to justify his arrest.

"What did he say against the government?" Pat asked.

The guard drew himself up, his back straight, his raised chin protruding in defiance. His large black eyes, bright with anger, were set in a broad ebony face, cold and hard. "Madam," he said. "This is a government matter!"

Pat turned away. She knew the guard was right. She was interfering in the affairs of a foreign government, in a matter which was none of her business. As an expatriate, she had no right to question motives or charges for arrests. Apparently, the case was developing into more than local jealousy. Tote-Man wasn't her responsibility; he had crossed her path, she respected him, and he was being treated unjustly. She was behaving in the way she had been taught; it was the American way. But Tote-Man was right. There was nothing she could do.

She started back home by the worn path. Looking back at the barracks-like building, she glanced at the small square window with horizontal bars where Tote-Man had been imprisoned. For a moment, she had the distinct impression she saw his face in shadows behind the bars. Thinking perhaps the heat might be playing tricks with her vision, she stopped and stared. Then she was sure.

She swallowed a hard lump in her throat and blinked to fight back tears. She hurried on, tired, trying to draw on memories from pleasant things back home—clean supermarkets with aisles of fruit and vegetables arranged in rows, spreading maples shading the clipped green lawn in front of her old Victorian house on a paved street, and her air-conditioned bedroom where she could sleep without fear of mosquitoes and malaria.

Catching sight of the red painted roof of her house in the distance between mango trees, she felt her legs too weak to carry her. She stopped beside the field spotted with ant hills shaped like mushrooms and sat in dust, a sagging lump, with one foot tucked under her, African style, the other extended for balance. Tears flowed down her sunburned face and dripped on dusty hands limp in her lap. The drone of flies hovering over the carcass of a decaying rodent beside the path was the only sound disturbing that torrid silence.

She stared at the small ant hills reminding her of fields of brown fungus and remembered reading that fungus was called "the life that follows death." Anger fired her determination; she wouldn't give up. She'd ask her husband to contact men with influence. She'd even pay for Tote-Man's release. If she couldn't work against the system, she would have to work within it like all the others, but the thought was as repulsive to her as swarming flies and odors of dried fish at the market.

THE STORM

Andrew didn't tell Sarah he wanted a divorce until they were already on their way to Lake Turkana and the Richard Leakey excavations at Koobi Fora. He was objective, business-like, as if talking to an employee about to be fired.

"I've been thinking about a separation for several months," he said. "I planned this trip to Kenya to get away, to see if anything would change that might save our marriage. I've decided it's best we separate and plan for a divorce."

They were sitting in black leather chairs at Wilson Airport in Nairobi; Sarah looked out over the runway, unprepared for what she heard him say.

"Did you hear what I said?" he insisted.

She stared at him and nodded, swallowing hard. "Is there someone else?"

"No, but I need space," he said. She didn't believe him.

"Maybe I'll never know what love is," he added after a pause.

"Let's talk about it when we get home," Sarah said. She didn't admit she hoped he would change his mind or that she'd ask him to see a marriage counselor.

They'd been married five years. Her mind raced back to the excitement of their wedding and the picture still hanging on the wall of their bedroom, her brown hair cascading shoulder-length under the veil, a tiara of pearls crowning her head, and Andrew, handsome in his tuxedo, his dark hair freshly styled for the wedding. They were smiling and embracing, and behind them the steeple of the old stone church glistened in sunlight; the photographer said he took his best pictures outdoors, and he was right. They were both beautiful and happy then. Sarah's couldn't believe their marriage would end like this.

They had met in college, played tennis together, studied side by side in the library, shared the worry of final exams. On school holidays he came to visit. Her parents liked him and encouraged the friendship. Sarah's father, a middle manager in a big corporation, had spoiled her with clothes, cars, college tuition, and her mother had taught her love and compassion. When she met Andrew, an orphan going to school on a scholarship, she sensed his hunger for affection. He clung to her, needed her, and he convinced her she would always be the most important thing in his life.

Sarah's father helped him get work with a friend in a money-management firm. The owner was pleased with his performance. They were so happy Sarah believed nothing could ever come between them, but when the money rolled in, and the children he wanted didn't arrive, he worked harder and worked more at night. Sarah went for numerous fertility tests, talked to Andrew about adopting a child and tried to show more affection to make up for the absence of children, but he expressed little interest in sex or social life. She joined clubs, took handicraft classes, carving out a place for herself while he worked. She accepted the pattern as one which might not change. Divorce was unthinkable. Her parents' marriage was a lasting one, and she thought hers would be the same.

Sarah wondered why Andrew chose a Nairobi airport to break the bad news. It seemed poor judgment to her, but he must have had a reason. He was a person who planned ahead, thought things through, and had a reason for almost everything he did. Rising anger told her to take a taxi back to town, but she'd always had such admiration for the Leakey family, she wanted this experience like no other. The trip to the Leakey excavations would be the grand finale to safaris in game parks, the visit to a Maasai village, and the champagne breakfast and balloon ride above Maasai Mara.

The Cessna soared north through morning sunlight, a trip of more than two hours. The uncommunicative pilot flew low along the Great Rift Valley, a three-thousand-mile fault stretching from the Red Sea to Mozambique, and in some places still looking as if the giant hand of God had sliced it with a knife. The deep valley was desert country, but land on top of the escarpment spread into acres of green cultivation dotted with white farmhouses. Sarah wanted to share what she saw with Andrew, but he sat on the other side of the plane, staring out the window, thinking his own thoughts. A heavy-set driver wearing a blue shirt and a straw hat met them in a Land Rover at the airport which was nothing more than a small strip of worn asphalt and dried grass with a room-sized tin shelter and a hand-printed welcome sign. Andrew helped transfer Sarah's luggage, but he seemed as distant as a stranger.

Recent rains had flooded the dirt road to the Lodge. The driver stopped where a group of men and women were fishing with ancient circular nets. Women packed fish into palm baskets. When Sarah tried to take a picture of the women, they howled in protest asking for money. They were accustomed to tourists and found them a rich source of supplementary income. Sarah put her camera away when the driver didn't offer to translate. A young African wearing a baseball cap, transferred them to a row boat for the remainder of the trip across the flooded area.

The cabins at Turkana Lodge looked primitive from a distance, but inside they were clean—linoleum floors, comfortable beds, cold and hot showers—and still smelled of disinfectant.

"Hum-m-m, twin beds," Andrew mused without looking at her. He tossed his luggage on a bed, opened the screen door, and said, "I'll see about arranging the trip to Koobi Fora for tomorrow."

From the small wooden porch, she watched him stroll down the concrete path between rows of dwarf palms toward the office. She was so used to his easy presence, his relaxed walk, the way his trousers fit over his slim hips, the shape of his head. A great sorrow trembled inside.

He returned sooner than she expected, saying the trip was uncertain, that the lodgekeeper had discouraged them from going. He said the Lake was dangerous that time of year; weather was unpredictable. After eating dinner in silence in the nearly empty dining room, they went to bed early without saying goodnight. Sarah lay awake, disappointed about the trip, disturbed, uncertain, fearful of the future. She remembered that during the past year their evenings were often shrouded in his silence, but she'd accepted this behavior as natural between couples who had grown comfortable with each other.

The sun rose radiant over the lake, and the sky was clear by morning. Weather reports were good. The lodgekeeper helped three men load the cabin cruiser outfitted with two outboard motors, fishing gear, a motorboat for fishing in coves, boxes of food, and sleeping bags. He warned the men to be off the lake as darkness fell when strong winds came up and cautioned them to keep in touch hourly by radio.

As the cruiser traveled north, water on the huge lake shimmered a jade green. The barren shore to the right, slanting steeply to a small mountain peak following the curve of the lake, was scattered with palms and scrub thorns. Among them sat tiny palm-leaf houses the color of sand.

Farther on, the cruiser stopped for fishing. When the guides helped Sarah pull in a Nile perch, its big head and round eyes glistening in sun, Andrew's face grew animated with excitement. He laughed and joked while bringing in his own catch and Sarah thought there might still be hope.

By late afternoon, they reached a small peninsula extending into the Lake. The guides made plans to go ashore for the night. They anchored the launch, transferred everyone to the small boat, and suggested Andrew and Sarah take off their shoes to wade through the swamp of sticky flamingo guano. A few yards away they stopped on a solid mud-flat, damp and smelling of mold; the men brought water to wash their feet and began to set up camp for the night.

"Where will we sleep?" Sarah asked.

"Here." The head guide, a small African in a plaid shirt, pointed to the mud, cold to her bare feet. She stared at him. They would be unprotected from night animals, including crocodiles.

Pointing to a shed-like building in the distance, she asked, "Why not there?"

"Too far to carry things."

Sarah looked at Andrew for support, but he was rummaging in his duffle-bag for a pair of dry shoes. He was deliberately trying to ignore her; she could expect no support from him.

"We will sleep there!" Sarah said. "I will help carry."

Grudgingly, the men carried the bags and cooking equipment to the building. Once inside, Sarah knew she had made a poor choice but was too embarrassed to admit it. The crude shelter was a mass of cobwebs and insect husks. They would be sleeping with spiders, lizards, and maybe scorpions. While the men cooked the Nile perch they had caught, she saturated the room with insect spray.

After dinner, only the faintest odor of insect repellent remained. She and Andrew spread their sleeping bags on the floor. They lay apart from each other in silence. Every syllable outside was audible; they could say nothing to each other that would not be overheard. She lay still, listening to zebras snort as they passed and to scavenger birds squawking for remains of their dinner. Night came down cold. Although they slept in their clothes, Sarah woke often to add extra layers.

Koobi Fora was a short distance across the Lake from the shelter. In prehistoric time, the land was part of Lake Turkana, but now it was bare sand, gravel, volcanic stone. The flat plain looked desolate and depressing spreading as far as Sarah could see with outcroppings of stone in the distance. Sarah felt she was looking at a moonscape— something foreign to anything she had ever known.

Francis, an African who had worked for the Leakeys for more than twenty years, met them in a Land Rover and drove across flat stretches of the ancient lake bed, his tire tracks the only signs of human habitation. He pointed out sediment millions of years old, showed them an ancient sea turtle, partially excavated and enclosed in a shelter to prevent damage from gushing rains. He drove to the outdoor museum sheltering a prehistoric mammoth. Here, primeval lapping waters had rounded the surface into gravely mounds; Sarah slipped, slid down one of the mounds, twisted her ankle. A guide helped her to her feet.

On their return to the boat, Francis stopped on a plain where numerous fossils had been washed to the surface by rains. He explained that with each heavy rain, a new layer of fossils was exposed. He pointed out how to identify them, but Sarah wasn't as interested as she thought she would be. Her ankle ached, and Andrew ignored her. She felt she was caught in a bad dream that wouldn't end.

She thought, "Here in this God-forsaken place with no doctors, no telephones, no hospitals, who cares if I sprain an ankle? Not the guides; I would remain a nuisance until they could collect their pay and leave. Maybe, after five years of sharing the same house, the same bed, the same breakfast table, not even Andrew!" She was terrified at the possibility and remembered reading that in the event of a death, the spouse was always the first person under suspicion. She felt uneasy.

Before leaving, they visited a small stone museum. Tall weeds and grass grew all around it. Most of the valuable specimens had been moved to Nairobi, but it held a few odd bones which the care-taker did not offer to identify and some charts which made little sense without explanation. A round-faced young man followed them, watched their every move, peeked around corners as if they might pocket a molar or some million-year-old fragment of mandible. Sarah couldn't hide her amusement. There was nothing in the place she wanted and she wouldn't have known what to do with it if she had it, but the man was meticulous about doing his job.

At noon, everyone settled in the motor launch ready to return to the Lodge. The "captain" drove at full speed for hours, then suddenly cut the motor. Two men boarded the small boat and paddled into a cove to fish for tilapia for meals at the Lodge. Andrew and Sarah were left with the third guide who tried to entertain them with fishing from the deck for nile perch. Their lines lay in water for more than an hour without a nibble. The guide spoke only when spoken to. Andrew lapsed into silence.

Sarah stared at the water and tried to comfort herself with the thought that within archaeological time, her problem was only a trifle, but that didn't ease the pain. Finally, she tried to pull in her line but caught it in Andrew's. She was afraid to look at him while the guide patiently untangled the knots.

"Let's go," she said. "It's late; the sun's going down." She remembered the lodgekeeper had warned them to be off the lake at sundown when strong winds came up. The guide signaled the fishermen with a mirror. The two men turned their motor on full speed, soon caught up, and boarded, bringing with them a wire cage of tilapia. They had waited too long. Before reaching shore, tropical darkness enveloped them. Cold night air descended on hot desert sand and warm lake water stirring a violent storm. A south wind roared about the launch as it cut into head wind. Great waves lifted the craft which skittered in spurts across the surface, rocking front to back, side to side. Guides held to the sides of the boat. The head guide talked into his hand-held radio, but his words were lost upon the wind. Sarah was thrown against Andrew; she grasped his hand, holding on tight. If the boat capsized, they could help each other struggle to shore. At least he owed her that much, but he brushed her hand away like a stinging insect.

Distant headlights of a Land Rover stationed to guide them ashore burned like feral eyes in light fog. That was the last thing Sarah remembered when a huge wave hit the launch and she was alone, trapped beneath the capsized boat. Floundering about, she found a small pocket of air, took a breath, and tried to dive, barely clearing the sides of the launch. Now her head was above water. She was not a good swimmer, but she managed to stay afloat. She looked about for Andrew and called his name, but her weak voice was swallowed by the wind. Sirens blasted from a rescue vehicle.

Sarah swam toward the lights on shore. Her uneasiness during the entire trip turned to full-blown panic as the storm tossed her about. The roar was disorienting; her ears ached. Slapping waves stung her face and tugged at her hair. She gasped for breath and swallowed lake water in big gulps when she tried to breathe with her mouth open. The water carried the bitter taste of minerals, mud, and algae. She thought about Andrew and of crocodiles sculling near shore waiting for prey. Her strength was almost gone when she saw the lodgekeeper swimming toward her with a life-preserver tied to a rope. He held her up while she pushed her head and arms through, and she let him pull her to shore.

She looked for Andrew and saw him standing with the guides drying his hair and neck with a towel. She started toward him, her long, stringy hair dripping over her face, her arms and body caked with mud. When their eyes met, she was shocked by the expression on his face and stopped short. Was it disappointment? Disgust? He turned his back. Chills took control of her body, and she shook so violently the lodgekeeper threw a blanket over her shoulders. She had seen on Andrew's face something she had not ever expected to see—complete rejection. He had wanted her dead. Yes, dead. Her disappearance would have solved so many problems for him—no divorce, no division of property, nothing. He would have been free. The turmoil in her mind crashed with the awful turbulence of the storm. For the first time in her life, she knew what it was like to be utterly and completely alone.

"Are you all right?" the lodgekeeper asked, his hand light on her shoulder.

"I'm all right," Sarah said, her teeth chattering.

"You were lucky," he said.

Yes, she thought, more lucky than you will ever know.

Sarah stumbled to her cabin to wash off any contamination from the lake. She vomited into the toilet. Then she took a shower and fell into bed, her hair still wet. She must have fallen asleep immediately as she did not hear Andrew when he came in.

Bright morning sun was shining through the window when she woke. Andrew's bed had been slept in, but he was not there. She went to the main lodge and found him in the courtyard behind the dining room where men squatted cleaning fish. Andrew had asked earlier about buying a Turkana spear, and someone had found a man willing to sell. There was something Neanderthal about the stocky, long-armed man dressed only in a loin cloth whose eyes beneath a sloping brow darted from Andrew to the men and back again. Sarah didn't have to know the language to understand they were scolding and encouraging him to bargain for a higher price than he had asked.

The lodgekeeper noticed Sarah standing at a distance. He strolled to her side, and spoke so softly the others could not hear.

"The men tell me you insisted on fishing too long. I warned you to be off the lake before dark. That was a bad thing for you to do; you could have drowned."

Sarah gasped and stared at him. So. The guides were placing the blame on her to save their jobs. And Andrew let them do it. Well, let them blame her. Nothing about the place mattered to her anymore.

She walked away for one last look at the lake before departure. When she saw workmen trying to salvage and clean the boat, she walked along the shore in the opposite direction. She needed to be alone to think about what to do. Turkana Lake was really a jade sea as some writers have said, but she was in no mood to be impressed. She didn't want to go back home with Andrew, but she had no choice, and she had the unsavory impression she had been used. She had been Andrew's means to a successful career; now he no longer needed her. She still needed him and wanted him, but she was afraid, terribly afraid, and felt vulnerable in a country where women have few legal rights.

A girl, dressed in a flowered skirt and ragged T-shirt, came from a village in a nearby field and walked beside her on a sandbar, her fingers weaving a palm-leaf basket as she walked. She spoke in fractured English telling about her missionary school, new English words she had learned, like "hobo" and "disk-jockey," and invited Sarah to her house to see handicrafts she had made. Sarah knew money was expected but followed her to that tiny palm hut, built like a bird's nest turned upside down, where the girl's only school book hung in a goatskin pouch from the center pole, and her mother's kitchen was a rack of sticks and driftwood, her stove a blackened hole in sand.

Bare-breasted village women pressed against Sarah begging her to buy baskets. The girl held up a doll she had made, saying, "My work is better." Sarah bought her Turkana doll, a stick of stained wood with a trace of the human figure dressed in a skirt of Nile-perch vertebrae strung like beads. The fish bones pricked her fingers when she accepted the doll. She watched the girl, almost a child, tie the coins she gave her in a dirty rag at her waist.

Flying home from Nairobi, Sarah asked to have her seat changed so she wouldn't have to ride beside Andrew.

"You didn't have to do that," he said. "We need to talk."

"We have nothing to talk about," Sarah said. His behavior at the Lake and his face had said everything she needed to know.

Later, she heard from a friend that Andrew's secret lover

bore him a son before the divorce was final. Now, when Sarah comes home from work at night exhausted and lonely, thinking of Andrew, she unwraps the doll from its tie-dyed cloth and lets the fish bones stick her fingers. . . reminding her how lucky she was to escape. She hasn't wanted to keep in touch, but she sometimes wonders if Andrew has found a better marriage, or if his distant, unloving ways, as cutting as the tip of the Turkana spear he brought back in his luggage, wounds the lives of other lonely women.

HOLIDAY

"Do we really have to go?" Cathy asked. Harold's hands were firm on the wheel and his jaw set like it always was when he'd made up his mind to do something. She looked sideways at his fine profile, almost delicate now that he'd lost weight, at his thinning brown hair and his sunburned nose too large for his face.

"The roads will be washed out from the long rains," she said."There will be gullies and potholes, and we might have to take the old VW in for repairs again." When Harold didn't answer, she persisted. "And we might get sick. We're not immune to all those things that don't affect village people."

"We have to go, Cathy," Harold said. His voice was sharp, edged with impatience. "I promised. But I told Elijah it would have to be a short visit." They rode in silence. "This will be a chance for you to see traditional Luo village life."

She knew he was right. During the six months they had lived in the Institute, she'd only heard about the ways of rural people.

Harold had arranged to meet Elijah Otieno in front of Whitfield's Bakery near the roundabout in Kisumu. He was to guide them to his village which was many kilometers off the tarmac road. Cathy was still thinking of excuses not to go. They had made reservations at a luxury hotel, The Sunset, with its gorgeous view of Lake Victoria. She wanted to lie around the pool or sit on the veranda looking at the lake. This was supposed to be a holiday. She understood why Harold felt obligated. Elijah was one of the most reliable workers in his water engineering unit at the Rift Valley Institute near Nakuru. He had been asking Harold for months to visit his village and his church in the Kakamega District. Like most workers at the Institute, he lived alone and had left his wife and children back in the village to work the *shamba*.

Cathy had met Elijah once when he dropped in unexpectedly at dinner. He was big for an African, well over six feet tall, of athletic build, and had a round, smiling baby-face incongruous with his rugged masculinity. He had greeted her shyly, almost obsequiously, and his voice was so soft she had to strain to understand his words through the mixture of thick British and Luo accents. He wore workers' soiled clothes, carried a heavy odor of sweat, and he wore one of those little white homemade caps identifying him as a member of the African Israel Nineveh Church of Kenya. Over a bowl of vegetable soup, which he sipped with obvious distaste, he talked gently with downcast eyes about his church, a charismatic sect which believes in miracles. He explained there was a huge stone near his house bearing letters carved upside down by the hand of God. His ancestors had discovered them at the top of this great stone when they migrated from the Upper Nile hundreds of years ago.

"They believed," he said, "this was a sign to settle there and God would return someday to finish the message."

"Do you believe that?" Cathy asked, incredulous.

"It is true," he said, nodding his head. "You must come to my house and see it. Yes. When can you come?"

From that time, Elijah had talked to Harold almost daily about religion and the stone with the message from God. He convinced Harold to visit his village to see the miracle for himself, while he, Elijah, was home on leave to entertain him properly.

They had agreed upon a day, and Cathy and Harold arrived at the bakery in Kisumu at noon to find Elijah lounging against the trunk of a giant cottonwood tree growing out of the sidewalk. The tall figure in the white cap was unmistakable even from a distance.

"You are late," he said with authority when they got out of the car to shake hands. "You said you would be here at eleven."

Cathy stared at Elijah; time was not a concept with which African usually concerned themselves. Images poured through her mind, images of Africans invited to dinner who wandered in two hours late, social events she'd attended starting three hours late, of appointments she'd kept on time when nobody showed up, and of repairmen who promised to come next day but came weeks later or not at all. Who was he, she wondered, to tell them they were late?

And there was another puzzling change. He looked them full in the face, smiled confidently, and shook hands, a subtle arrogance in his straight shoulders and the tilt of his head. Cathy cringed with humiliation when Harold responded to him meekly.

"We didn't get away as soon as we expected."

Cathy immediately got into the front seat of the car and motioned Elijah to get in back. The transformation in him made her uneasy. She had no intention of sitting in the back seat, silent and obedient, like a traditional African woman.

They drove ten kilometers on the tarmac road toward Kakamega. Behind them, Lake Victoria lay in mist against the horizon like a wide expanse of sky. On either side, giant boulders scattered in careless piles spotting rugged terrain. Hills and small mountains with outcroppings of stone, smoothed and rounded from millions of years of erosion, were grim reminders of volcanic action and violent geologic upheavals in a prehistoric past. On steep inclines, mud huts with thatched roofs nestled among boulders, as much a part of nature's design as the scattered wattle, sisal, and twisted thorn. At times, the harsh reality of huts beside scorched and stunted *shambas* of maize was softened by the presence of a full-bodied mango tree or a leafy, palm-like papaya.

"Take this road," Elijah called.

Harold turned off the tarmac and drove toward the hills. The rutted and pot-holed dirt road was washed out by torrential rains which had come too early to benefit the maize crops.

As Harold eased the VW around deep pits and gullies, Cathy hoped he would heed her warning about damaging the car, but he gave no indication he remembered.

From the back seat, Elijah continued to direct their progress along roads seldom traveled by vehicles. Narrow wild growth of thorny hedge crowded in on either side, scratching the sides of the car, flipping into open windows. They rolled up the windows and watched the windshield fog. Meanwhile, Elijah barked orders from the back: "Right!". . . "Left!". . . "Turn here!"

After jolting and weaving around miles of washouts, they came upon a thatched mud-brick primary school where children played games in the school yard. Elijah directed Harold to leave the road and drive through the school grounds. Crowds of children followed the car yelling, squealing, and taunting, "*Mzungu!*" "*Mzungu!*" and ran beside the car until it was on the road again. Elijah smiled and waved. One feisty boy chased them down the road and threw a stone which skidded between the wheels.

"*Mzungu*?" Cathy asked of Elijah. "Is that a bad word?"

He laughed. "It means white people."

Cathy had been told that *mzungu* was a derogatory word,

but she wanted Elijah to confirm or deny it and know she understood.

She wondered why he told Harold to drive through the school yard as the gullies on the playground were as deep as those on the road. Elijah looked back and waved again at the children. Cathy was embarrassed. He had wanted to look important to local children, to have them see him riding in a car. It seemed such a childish thing for him to do.

Beyond the school, the roads disintegrated into little more than a path scattered with large round boulders. Harold eased the old VW over them, scraping as he maneuvered from one side to the other. Vegetation on either side of the path had been chopped. Cathy imagined Elijah, his brothers, nephews, and other village men swinging *pangas* to clear the road for their visit. Along the path, village women carrying water jugs or bags of produce on their heads turned to watch, their eyes wide. Barefoot children in soiled, tattered shirts and dust-caked dresses appeared, their huts barely visible behind the bushes of yellow thorn.

Within sight of Elijah's homestead, they were confronted with two huge boulders on either side of the road—boulders the size of small huts. The narrow space between them had been filled with fresh, moist earth, also more evidence of the prodigious amount of work in preparation for their visit. Harold stopped.

"I'll have to leave the car here," he said.

"You can go!" Elijah said, anxiety in his voice. "You can go!"

"I'll wreck my car," Harold said.

"You can go!" he insisted. Then he added quietly, "I do not trust these people." He indicated a group of young men who were following behind.

Cathy had heard that rural people could be trusted, that stealing or other deviant behavior was restrained by harsh tribal punishment. She knew by Elijah's voice he intended to have his way; there had to be some other reason.

Harold revved the engine and plowed through, the sides of the car scraping only slightly.

"Now park in front of my house," he ordered.

At last Cathy was beginning to understand. He wanted curious friends and relatives who came to gawk at them to know his visitors were important enough to own a car, and for his own prestige, he wanted the car parked in front of his hut.

Cathy recognized the hut arrangement as one of the traditional Luo villages she'd read about in books. The huts were built in a circle with the father's hut in a central location, the wives' and sons' huts completing the circle. Elijah's father had recently died; his gravestone stood nearby in the shade of a towering jackfruit tree. As the first wife's eldest son, Elijah was now in charge of family affairs.

When their car stopped in front of Elijah's hut, a crowd surged forward. Cathy counted nineteen children and fourteen adults. They had to shake hands all around, a time-consuming ritual. Each family member was introduced by a Biblical name such as Tobias, Noah, Jonah, Shadrach, Esther, Leah, and Mary. They were dressed in church clothes in honor of the occasion with the insignia of the church on sleeves or pockets.

After introductions, a group of men sat in wooden, homemade chairs to weave baskets. Fingers worked furiously tucking brittle field grass around uneven bunches of stems held in the form of a cross. They chatted earnestly in Luo. Jacob, a young man home on leave from work in Nairobi, translated.

"He wants you to take his photo making baskets," he said, indicating an elderly uncle who was blind.

When Harold brought out his camera to take pictures, all the men present crowded around the chair. Cathy knew the faces would be little more than dark blurs. People came running, arranging themselves in groups. Women wanted to be photographed with husbands, mothers with babies, men with sons. There were family portraits, group pictures of children, photographs with friends. Eijah stood nearby smiling, deciding which photographs would be taken with his hut and the car in the background.

"They want you to send prints," Jacob said.

Elijah nodded. "Of course. You must send prints."

When there seemed to be no more photographs to take, Harold asked, "Can we see the big stone now?"

"Not yet," Elijah said. "You must see my house."

The name of his church, "African Israel Nineveh" was painted above the door. The square hut was built of clay and cow dung skillfully smoothed to look like painted concrete. Elijah pointed out that his house was the best in the village.

Inside, the hut was divided into two rooms. The parlor was lined with homemade chairs. Small wooden tables in front of each chair were covered with white crocheted spreads. "My wife, Mary, made them," Elijah said, pointing to the crocheted cloths. A tray of soft drinks sat on a table by the door. Elijah took a bottle opener out of his pocket and opened the drinks with a flourish. He asked Cathy and Harold to sit, offered them warm cokes, saying, "Soon we will see the big stone."

Cathy and Harold followed Elijah and a group of children up a rough narrow path among growth of thorn bush pushing in on either side. In the distance lay a chain of hills, rounded boulders, rocky ledges, tufts of twisted trees. They passed mud huts tucked among bushes where men were making baskets. Small children ran out to meet them, laughed at their white faces, and followed in pied-piper fashion up the hill. Soon they came to a clearing and saw the tall boulder loom ahead. It stood alone with no other outcropping of rock nearby. A square mud hut, not yet finished, sat at the base of the rock, a small wooden cross above the door.

"This is our church," Elijah said. "We built it here." His long arm swept upward toward the stone, "and this is where God will come when he finishes writing that word."

Indistinct markings were scrawled across the granite stone. Cathy thought one could, with an active imagination, read them as upside-down letters.

"Look!" Elijah said. "Only God could do that. No person can climb there. Do you agree?"

Cathy noticed two teenage boys climbing up through the cracks in the tall stone. Through these cracks, it might be possible to reach the top. It wasn't likely anyone would go to the trouble to make upside-down letters on that stone, but it was possible. She thought the marks were more likely made by abrasions from land upheavals in prehistoric time when another rock formation split away.

"But what does it mean?" Harold asked.

"The word is not finished," Elijah said. "Can you see the R and the L? And there on the side is a big D."

"Will the message be in Luo?" Harold asked.

"We do not know," he said, "but we will know when God comes with his message." He stood looking up at the stone with pride and wonder.

"Now," he said. "You must take photos and then we will go up the mountain."

While Harold took church pictures and talked with Elijah, the children lost interest and returned the way they came.

Again Cathy and Harold followed Elijah up a rocky mountain path, struggled among huge boulders, stumbled up ledges of sheer rock. Along the way, baboons grumbled and scolded from a distance. Lean nursing mothers peered around ledges and disappeared behind jagged rocks. Eventually, Elijah stood on a great boulder of bare granite. He helped Cathy and Harold to the top where Lake Victoria spread in an endless stretch of water to the south, merging with gray sky, and the city of Kisumu was barely visible to the left. Cathy found the view magnificent. Nobody spoke. At that moment, she understood why ancient prophets went to mountain tops to pray, to find God, to rise above the shabbiness of little men. She felt wind tugging at her hair and clothes as if trying to coax her into the spirit world. Watching mist blow off the lake, shrouding everything in mystery, she stood silent and humbled.

The men in the compound were still weaving baskets when they returned. A dozen or more baskets were stacked beside the blind man. They were shallow and poorly finished around the rim.

"Why are they making so many baskets?" Harold asked Elijah.

"The maize crop has failed," he said, pointing to the yellow stunted fields of maize surrounding the compound. Soon there will be much hunger. We must sell them at the market to buy food."

"How many shillings will they get for one basket?"

"Five," he said. That is not much but it will keep away hunger."

Harold looked at his watch. "We have to go now. We are expected back at the hotel."

"You cannot go," Elijah said.

Harold laughed, "But we have to."

"You cannot go," Elijah repeated. "My wife is cooking for you."

"We don't wish to trouble her," Harold said, "and we need to get back to the hotel."

Elijah said quietly, "You cannot go until you eat."

Cathy was exhausted from the trek up the mountain and wanted to get back to the hotel for a nap. She resented his insistence, but she knew they couldn't go without Elijah to guide them back to the main road. She looked about and saw no evidence of food being served any time soon except for a woman squatting behind a bush washing dishes in a pan of dirty water.

While men talked with Harold, Joseph led Cathy to a small gathering of women. Elijah's mother, Sara, had arranged chairs under the jackfruit tree. She had stationed Jonah, one of her grandsons who worked in Nairobi, to sit beside her and act as interpreter. "She wants to know if you like roasted maize," he asked.

"Very much," Cathy said. She had eaten it once at a roadside stand, hot from the wire grill. Jonah relayed the message and she sent a boy to roast an ear of maize on the charcoal *jiko*.

"She wants to know if you will send her a dress from the United States," Jonah said.

Cathy paused, searching for a response that wouldn't be offensive. "Tell her I could send her a dress, but she would have to pay many shillings in duty to get it from the post office."

They spoke in Luo while she waited, trying to glean meaning from their tones and facial expressions.

Finally Jonah asked, "What is duty?"

Cathy explained what she knew of Kenyan duty and customs laws and tried to explain why the government discouraged imports.

"How much would she have to pay?" Jonah asked.

"Many shillings," Cathy said. "She would do better to buy a dress in the market from people who sell used clothing."

Sara looked thoughtful while Jonah explained, then he said, "She says she can see the fault is on this side." After a pause, he continued. "She has no money. She wants you to give her money to buy a dress."

"I have no money with me," Cathy said. Harold had brought money with him, but Cathy hadn't carried her purse.

"She says Americans are rich and you can get the money," Jonah said.

The child brought the ear of roasted maize. Cathy thanked him and tried to change the subject.

"You have a nice house," Cathy said to Sara. She pointed to the square hut with a tin roof.

"It's not nice," Sara said, shaking her head. "The house needs a new roof. Water drips inside during the rainy season," She paused while her grandson translated and then added. "Can you help me get a new roof?" Cathy knew how costly corrugated tin roofs could be. She and Harold had been helping their cook get one at the rate of two sheets per month.

"Why doesn't she make a roof of tall grass?" Cathy asked. "I think thatched roofs are nice."

"She says the grass must be collected from far away. It's too far for her to walk."

Cathy wanted to ask why her grandsons couldn't help her, but that might have been rude as men were not expected to carry burdens.

An elderly woman came out of a hut and sat in a chair beside Cathy. She wasn't sure, but she thought the woman might be Joseph's mother, Elijah's father's second wife. The woman wore a soiled blue flowered dress and a blue sweater hanging in shreds about her shoulders. She spoke earnestly with Jonah who shook his head and seemed to argue with her about something.

Finally, Jonah laughed and looked embarrassed. "Old people think the way to be friendly with Europeans is to ask for a gift," he said. "It goes back to their relationship with the British."

Elijah came by with a tray of warm coke. Harold stood behind Cathy's chair with his camera slung over his shoulder.

"Please, let's go," she whispered.

He shook his head and frowned. "We can't. We have to stay."

Cathy watched Harold wander off to take more photographs. She felt trapped.

The food finally came. There was a big discussion about what to do with Cathy as men and women didn't eat together. Finally, Cathy and Harold were invited into Elijah's house where Cathy ate with Harold and two elderly men, but it was awkward. The men looked embarrassed, stared at the floor, and nobody talked. After they rinsed their hands in a basin of water brought in by a young girl, Elijah's wife served boiled rice and fish in a curry sauce. Village men ate with their hands, but Elijah gave serving spoons to Cathy and Harold.

Cathy thought the meal skimpy, but it had taken many hours to cook on the charcoal jiko. She liked neither fish nor curry, but knew Elijah was trying to impress them by serving rice instead of maize. She tried to be polite and eat as much as she could, but the food lay heavy on her stomach. Then Elijah served a strong tea boiled in milk. She wondered if there had been enough food for everyone, or if she and Harold and the village elders in the room with them were getting special treatment. While Elijah was out of the room, Cathy asked again about leaving.

"The roads are so bad, we ought to get out of here before dark."

Harold shrugged. "Apparently Elijah has planned entertainment for us. We can't go until he's ready. He'd lose face with his people."

If the village elders understood the conversation, they gave no notice of it, but Cathy didn't care. She felt like a captive.

In late afternoon, Elijah led his household up the path to the church to hold a service for Harold and Cathy. Other families joined them along the way. The wooden benches were almost filled. Elijah gave the first part of the service in English. He talked about the sacred stone where God had left his unfinished message and how God would return through his son so everybody would know the truth. He read from Thessalonians telling how God would increase the faith of the good people and protect them from evil people and evil spirits, and he told how to prepare for the second coming. They sang old religious songs in Luo; Cathy recognized some of the tunes from her childhood. Then he followed the singing with a sermon in Luo for his people, his face was radiant, his arms flailed, his voice rose to a fervent cry sometimes falling to a faint whisper. The people listened intently, some cried out, others clapped. At the end of the sermon, everyone filed out of church into twilight to stand in a circle before the sacred stone.

A dancer came out of the dark wearing a grotesque mask and costume—raffia skirt, a crocheted and beaded blouse, and a headdress of twine and shells. He danced furiously in the center of the circle to the throbbing beat of drums. Cathy's gaze followed the eyes of the crowd fixed on a fire at the top of the stone, a light as if from a campfire. Everybody stood transfixed gazing at the light.

"That is an evil spirit," Jonah whispered in Cathy's ear. "Are you afraid?"

Cathy shook her head. "Why is the man dancing?"

"He is dancing away the evil spirit. When the evil spirit is gone, he will stop."

Soon the light disappeared, the dancing stopped, and the crowd walked down the hill singing a lilting song in Luo. People who had joined them on the way up, fell by the wayside, drifting to their own huts and homesteads.

Cathy held Harold's arm, but she stumbled often and felt as if the thorn bushes were reaching out for her. Her eyes were not accustomed to dark, and she still felt dizzy from the unreal effects created by the drums and dancing.

Back at his house, Elijah was ready for them to leave. Cathy and Harold went through the long ritual of shaking hands. Harold gave Elijah's mother and his wife one hundred shillings each. His mother squealed her happiness; now she could buy a dress. Elijah's wife accepted the money without comment. People in the crowd tried to extract a promise from them to come again. Then the requests began: one man wanted a ride to Nakuru next day, another wanted a ride to the main road to visit a friend, another wanted Harold to take him to Nairobi for business. There seemed to be no end.

Elijah reprimanded them in Luo, and he and his friend, Isaac, who lived in a village on the other side of the tarmac road, climbed in the back seat to give Harold directions. The moon was just coming up behind tall trees, but the night was dark. Cathy sat shivering in the front seat praying silently they would not be stranded in the bush in a battered car in a country she didn't understand.

Easing across the last big gully, the car rattled, scraped, made strange noises. When Harold reached the smooth surface of the tarmac, he got a flashlight from beneath the seat and looked under the car.

"It's the muffler," he said, "and the exhaust pipe is broken. We may be able to make it back to the hotel."

Elijah and Isaac laughed, shook hands, and disappeared in darkness toward Isaac's village.

Cathy tried not to, but she couldn't control feelings of resentment toward Elijah for leaving his wife with the cleaning after feeding a multitude, and for leaving Harold with a damaged car.

Cathy didn't talk to Harold all the way back to the hotel. She was exhausted, her stomach felt queasy, and she still had the impression of being held against her will.

Still not speaking, they took the elevator to their room. They didn't bother to glance out the patio doors at the moonlit view of Lake Victoria.

Harold undressed and stood naked before her, pulling a blue bathing suit over his hips.

"I'm going down for a quick swim before the pool closes," he said."Maybe I'll sleep better."

Cathy didn't offer to go. "I'm going to have a drink," she said. "It may make me sick, but I'm going downstairs for a drink." Cathy didn't like alcohol, but it seemed the safest way of rebelling against the situation.

She went to the lounge and ordered a glass of wine. It had a strange, bitter taste. She went back to the room without drinking it.

Harold was already there. "I was too sick to swim," he said.

Cathy knew how he felt. She had stomach pains, a headache, and her eyes smarted. She tried to recall everything they had touched or eaten. The food had been thoroughly cooked, but were the plates clean? They drank cokes out of bottles, no water, and the tea had been boiled. They had shaken hands with everybody; maybe that was it, or was it the evil spirit?

Harold put on his pajamas and went to bed, groaning a little. He lay with his eyes closed, and Cathy knew he was trying not to be sick. She dressed for bed and went out on the balcony to see the moon over the lake, but a cluster of clouds had settled over it. She went to bed disappointed.

Cathy woke during the night violently ill. She went out on the balcony for fresh air. She was too nauseated to sleep and she was angry. She was angry with Harold for taking her to the village. She felt guilt and anger for not being able to give the women things they'd asked for. She was angry with Elijah for using them to show off his position of importance. She felt disgusted and angry with herself for taking part in something that seemed unclean, something not quite honest. And beyond her anger, there was a dull penetrating ache, a silent grieving for the village people and basket makers who would soon know hunger. She felt weak and powerless, knowing her perception of people and the world would never again be the same.

On the lake, the light from the boat dock and the light from the moon intercepted, casting a cross over the water. An eddy of wind caressed her hair, cooled her cheeks. She stood looking up at the sky, brilliant with stars and wondered if somewhere in that expanse of limitless space, there were other inhabited planets, and if there were other gods who wrote indecipherable messages on blocks of weathered stone.

A Far Country

Victoria enters the village through a corridor of bamboo. The July heat in the middle of the dry season has turned the stalks and leaves a luminous yellow. They rattle like chimes in the breeze. She wipes her sweating hands on her cotton skirt and twists the ends of her long hair the tropical sun has bleached a golden taffy. Dust grits between her toes inside the cheap plastic sandals. She is thinking of her parents and of Andrew, the boyfriend she left behind, and she wants to go home. "Two years is a long time," he had said. "Do you think our relationship is strong enough to last that long?"

Since childhood, she has wanted to be a Peace Corps teacher. A year ago, she came to the village with Donna and Richard, enthusiastic and with high expectations, but now she knows she is not prepared for the emotional strain of the work she has to do. She feels committed to finish her two-year contract but wonders if her commitment is fear of failure. She remembers a mountain climber once said to her, "The best mountain climber doesn't always go to the top."

Her shoulders ache with fatigue. Her day at the school near Kolozana village has been long, hot and stressful with too few books and materials for the children. She passes a hand over her forehead as if to brush away her headache. Her face feels hot. She wonders if she has malaria again, but she tries not to think about it.

Ahead of her she sees a cluster of round huts thatched with

maudze grass, blending naturally with the landscape. Her eyes search for Malia, her favorite person in the village. Malia sits on the ground in front of her hut, her legs extended and the thick soles of her feet calloused and cracked. Her soiled blue head cloth frames her round face. She is husking a basket of maize, her chant almost a whisper. She waves an ear of maize at Victoria and smiles.

Victoria moves toward her, picking her way through scrawny straw-colored chickens pecking at maize chaff in the dust. She sits on the clay porch Malia built around her circular bamboo hut, cups her chin in both hands and rests her elbows on her knees. Malia smiles at her and makes a purring sound low in her throat. They sit in silence while Malia shells maize and Victoria watches the village.

Haunting notes of a bamboo flute drift through the clear air—a chant as basic as a warbler calling from its perch on the *mwabvi* tree. A boy sits in the door of the boys' hut playing a flute. His fingers glide over the rough apertures, the toes on his huge adolescent feet curl upward as he plays, and his eyes rest on a dream in the distance. He made the flute himself, and he has made other musical instruments—a ground harp, a bamboo frame filled with maize for shaking, a drum from a hollow log. He has promised to make a flute for her to take home on the plane, saying he does not want her to forget him.

Victoria watches two girls, barely toddlers, start a fight over a tin can and a gourd doll. They settle the argument by staring at each other then walk away. She is amazed at the lack of conflict in the village, especially among children, as she remembers the tough-and-tumble fist fights, hair pulling, and scratching among her cousins and nephews at home. A group of boys from her school gather under a big tree to tie knots into string, making traps for catching birds. Another is weaving a small practice mat with strips of bamboo. Others zigzag through the village on a wooden "hotrod" the headman made for a toy. They squeal and push each other near Victoria inviting her approval.

Malia points to a jagged hole in the abandoned hut beside them. Loni, a small boy squatting inside, watches Victoria through the hole. After school, he follows her about the village staring with worship in his large round eyes. He's almost old enough to go to school but has no speech. He lives with his grandmother, Avalisi, who cannot feed him. Every night he sits in the dust beside Victoria's table waiting for her to share food. He has been sick from infancy with mouth fungus and rashes. A Canadian researcher at Kadende Village takes him to the government health clinic once a month in his Land Rover where they wait in line for hours to see a "doctor" who is a trained technician, a practical nurse, and a sweeper who changes bandages. Loni tugs on Victoria's skirt when it's time for his medicine.

"Good evening." Victoria recognizes the cheerful voice calling to her in English. It is Juma, an orphan in the village. She teaches him to read after school. The headman's wife gives him food, but nobody can pay his school fees. He carries the tattered reader she bought for him. He has learned faster than any child she has ever known, but he is already too old to be accepted in government schools. He reads while she listens, corrects his errors, and then talks to him about the story. She promises to teach him math tomorrow, but today she is too tired.

"Madam," he says. When he addresses her formally, Victoria knows he is going to ask for something. "Will you bring me a new book from school?"

"There are not enough books for the students," she says, "but when I go to Chipata next month, I will buy books especially for you."

Juma smiles, his eyes shining, his dimples growing deeper. "Someday, I will go to school."

Victoria feels her throat constrict and tears sting her eyes. She is determined not to cry. She lets him walk away dreaming his impossible dream.

She watches the afternoon sun slide behind the tops of trees casting shadows across the village yard. Simon, the headman's blind brother, walks out of the bamboo grove on his way back to the village. She had seen him stride before her on the way to school in early morning, feeling his way with his stick, his thin legs like pegs stuck into his only pair of too-big shoes. From a distance, he reminds Victoria of a skinny little boy playing dress-up in his father's clothes. He was blinded by smallpox when he was a child and sent to Maguero Mission School for the blind to learn to read and write in braille. Now he is the only adult in the village who can read.

Children run to meet him and follow to the door of his hut. They wait while he removes his shoes and deacon's coat and comes out carrying his braille board. He sits on the ground between Malia and Victoria adjusting the braille board in his lap. Somehow he knows Victoria is there, and she knows he will ask her questions and take notes. Children and women gather to listen. After greeting her, he asks, "Are there schools for the blind in your country?"

"In the cities, there are many."

"Will you give me the address of a school for the blind in America?"

"Most schools are for children," she says, "but I will try to get an address of a school with services for adults."

"I want to write to a school in America," Simon says. "I want to go there to learn English." Victoria stares at the shades of brown in the bare village yard. She does not want to disappoint him, but it would be wrong to give him hope. She sees Malia and the other women shake their heads, exchange knowing looks, and smile.

"Is it expensive to travel to America?" he asks after a long silence.

"Yes, very expensive."

"I went to Chipata today to ask about borrowing money," Simon says. "Did you pay as much as thirty *kwacha*?

"Much more."

"More than a hundred?"

"More than a thousand."

"Is it far to your country?"

"Yes, very far."

"How far?"

"Thousands of miles."

"How many hours did you travel to get here?"

"I was without sleep three days and two nights."

"Did you come by boat or airplane?"

"Airplane."

"Then it must be very far indeed!"

Above the clatter of the braille board, Malia and the women giggle, shake their heads and scoff.

"You are a foolish old man," Malia says.

"How can you expect to go to America when you have no money?" says another.

"Who will feed you and take care of you when you leave this village?"

"Who will wash your clothes?"

"Who will cook your *nsima*?"

"Who will carry your bath water?"

They laugh, gurgling sounds interspersed with cackles of derision. They slap their knees.

"That is a good joke!" Malia says, laughing. The others nod in agreement.

Victoria does not want to hear their cruel words and wishes she did not understand Nyanja. She is disappointed in Malia.

"You must be very rich," Simon says.

"No," Victoria says. "My government pays for everything."

Simon hangs his head, his shoulders slump, his unseeing eyes stare at the ground. He has been needlessly humiliated.

"Perhaps I can find someone in this country to teach you English," Victoria says gently.

Simon shakes his head. "It would not be the same."

Victoria watches him go, feeling his way back to his hut with the stick he uses for a cane. She does not believe he will live long. He is thin. He eats barely enough to sustain life because he cannot do his share of work. And now he has no dream!

Victoria hears a baby cry and knows it is Nyasi. Chewa babies are usually contented babies, but not Nyasi. Chewa babies are nursed at the first cry of hunger and carried on their mother's backs, but not Nyasi. He is Loni's baby brother whose mother is in South Africa with her new husband, and Nyasi is too young to wean. His grandmother, Avalisi, is sick and cannot care for him properly. He needs maize porridge, thin and well-cooked, and clean vegetables cooked into mush, but his grandmother cannot carry firewood; she eats what other people give her. Nyasi needs milk, but tsetse flies kill cattle, and there is no money to buy milk. Nursing mothers in the village have no milk to share. Nyasi cries when other babies play and stumbles about the village on wobbly legs.

Victoria watches Avalisi leave the village with a clay pot on her head. She must get water from the well before dark, and she cannot carry Nyasi with her. Nyasi follows her out the door with a slow, unsteady gait, but he is too weak to go with her to the well. He stands outside and howls, his head thrown back in protest of being left alone in a big and confusing world. He stumbles near a sick dog which was bitten by a baboon and is dying of paralysis. Victoria fears for his safety. Suddenly, the headman's elderly mother hobbles from her hut, and, walking without haste on twisted limbs, draws Nyasi to safety.

Avalisi returns from the well as Nyasi stands crying beside the cold gray ashes from yesterday's cooking fire. Powdery ends of half-burned sticks point in all directions near his small brown feet. His toes grip the hard-packed earth. His dust-caked shirt does not cover his tiny penis. His face is abandoned to childhood's uninhibited misery as he raises one bony arm pleading for help. Avalisi brushes past him, clucking her affection. A beige puppy from the hunting dog lifts its ears to Nyasi's loud cries and rubs against his legs as if to caress and comfort. In Victoria's feverish state, Nyasi seems to represent all of Africa, begging to be saved from the human condition.

Night's darkness has erased Malia; there is no moon. Victoria moves beside her and shells an ear of maize as if the few grains falling through her fingers could make Malia's life easier. She remembers her first few days in the village when she sat beside Malia watching her feed her baby chunks of *nsima* dipped in a paste of wild greens. She had watched as Malia settled the baby on her back and reached for an ear of maize, placing it in a shallow basket at Victoria's feet. Victoria had helped her shell maize into the basket, and she had felt a communion, a spiritual closeness she had not known before. Malia had tapped the side of a large square basket with an ear of maize.

"*Chitundu*," she said with authority.

"*Chitundu*," Victoria repeated.

Then Malia tapped the shallow basket used for winnowing.

"*Lichero*," she said, making the R sound like an L.

"*Lichero*," Victoria said.

"*Chimanga*," Malia called, shaking an ear of maize in moonlight.

"*Chimanga*," Victoria said obediently.

Then Malia had thrust dry husks into her hands. She saw their outlines in pale light and felt their crisp, coarse texture against her skin.

"*Khoko*," Malia said, holding up one maize husk. Without responding, Victoria gathered a load of husks in her arms and said in a loud voice, "*Makhoko!*" They both laughed.

Victoria still remembers the musical notes of approval singing low in Malia's throat as they shelled in silence, listening to muted voices floating across the village. She still remembers that indescribable oneness she felt with Malia on that night, the bright stars, the complete and satisfying peace. She wants to recapture that feeling of quiet harmony by sitting with Malia again to shell maize, but it does not return. She has seen too much pain, sorrow, cruelty, beyond her power to ease, and she wants to go home to soft beds, mellow bedside lamps, her collection of books and records, and to Andrew. When she leaves, she knows she will never forget the taste of wood smoke from cooking fires, a sweet odor saturating her clothes, a fragrance she will carry home in her luggage. She will miss the murmur of parents and grandparents putting children to bed, and laughter from the boys' hut as adolescents whisper secrets.

Malia says she must put her children to bed and stands to say goodnight. When their hands clasp, the callouses on Malia's palms burn into Victoria's memory. She carries the sensation with her as she gropes her way through darkness to her hut. Fatigue is heavy across her shoulders, her arms ache, pain presses against her eyes and the back of her head. She touches her forehead and wonders if she has a temperature. Does she have sleeping sickness this time?

She feels for the flashlight inside the door of her hut. The single ray of light makes a yellow circle in her suitcase where she finds the thermometer. She hears the click of glass against her teeth as she shoves it into her mouth. The thermometer is cold against her lips. Without undressing, Victoria crawls into the sleeping bag spread out on the old army cot she brought with her to the village. She is thinking that tomorrow she will send a message to the Canadian researcher at Kadende village to come for her and take her to the Mission Hospital. She falls asleep with the thermometer under her tongue.

Nyasi is crying and Juma is calling her name. "Victoria. Victoria," he chants in precise syllables. Victoria rises, drifts to the grass door, pushes it open. The night is dark, but Juma, Nyasi, and Loni stand in a flood of white light. Loni's swollen face expands like a balloon. She opens her mouth to scream, but the sound burns in her throat. Nyasi stands, uplifted arms, a silent scream on his baby-face. Simon is suddenly there, his grotesque features illuminated with a glow of yellow light streaming through bamboo. His long, thin fingers guide the click of the braille board. Juma is reading aloud, looks up, his dimples deep as wounds. "We love you Victoria," his voice a hollow echo. "I love you, too," Victoria tries to say, but the words will not come. She holds out her arms as Juma drifts beyond her reach. "You cannot touch us," he says in perfect English. His voice vibrates, echoes, fades away. "We live in a different time, a different place." They disappear. . . the night is black. "Come back! Come back!" Victoria screams. "I need you." She feels herself falling, a particle of light streaking weightless through the universe to a frightening, unknown death.

Victoria groans and wakes slowly. Her arms and legs are numb, her heart pounds, her clothes are wet with sweat. She thinks she hears the notes of a bamboo flute, or the cry of a small animal—she cannot be sure. Perhaps that, too, is part of her dream. She lies in dark, shivering, thinking of Loni, Nyasi, Juma, and Simon, knowing she has no power to save them. She has decided to go home; even here she lives in a far country where they cannot go.

About the Author

Stacy Johnson Tuthill completed ***The Taste of Smoke*** with the encouragement of a Works-in-Progress grant from the Maryland State Arts Council. She was awarded a fellowship for poetry by the Maryland State Arts Council for poems in her book ***Pennyroyal*** (1991) now used in various public schools. Her most recent book, ***Necessary Madness*** (1992) won the University of Alaska, Fairbanks, chapbook award. She was born in Kentucky and earned degrees at the University of Kentucky and the University of Illinois. She has lived in Sierra Leone, Kenya, and Zambia where she won a chapbook contest sponsored by the Ministry of Culture. Her work has been published in numerous anthologies and literary magazines. She has read at USIS in Lusaka, Zambia, the Folger Shakespeare Library, the Smithsonian Institution, the Writer's Center in Bethesda, for local television and other places in Maryland, Virginia, and Washington, D.C. She taught literature, advanced composition, and creative writing in Maryland for twenty years and lives with her husband near the University of Maryland campus.